Christina reached over.

"Your collar was distracting me," she said, her voice throaty.

Different from the normally clipped, professional tone of Christina Mendoza, business analyst.

But now, she was just a woman.

And he was a man.

Alone together on a Saturday night.

He didn't even breathe for fear of reminding her that her fingertips were still brushing his collar. The heat of her skin lingering so close to his neck turned him inside out, exposing a side of himself he always kept locked away.

Did she see the unguarded desire in his eyes? The terrifying curiosity of wanting to know what it was like to be with a woman who had great substance?

Maybe she did because, before his heart could beat again, she'd pulled away, stood and walked toward her computer.

Dammit, why hadn't he made a move on her?

Dear Reader,

Get ready to counter the unpredictable weather outside with a lot of reading *inside*. And at Silhouette Special Edition we're happy to start you off with *Prescription: Love* by Pamela Toth, the next in our MONTANA MAVERICKS: GOLD RUSH GROOMS continuity. When a visiting medical resident—a gorgeous California girl—winds up assigned to Thunder Canyon General Hospital, she thinks of it as a temporary detour—until she meets the town's most eligible doctor! He soon has her thinking about settling down—permanently....

Crystal Green's *A Tycoon in Texas*, the next in THE FORTUNES OF TEXAS: REUNION continuity, features a workaholic businesswoman whose concentration is suddenly shaken by her devastatingly handsome new boss. Reader favorite Marie Ferrarella begins a new miniseries, THE CAMEO— about a necklace with special romantic powers—with *Because a Husband Is Forever*, in which a talk show hostess is coerced into taking on a bodyguard. Only, she had no idea he'd take his job title literally! In *Their Baby Miracle* by Lilian Darcy, a couple who'd called it quits months ago is brought back together by the premature birth of their child. Patricia Kay's *You've Got Game*, next in her miniseries THE HATHAWAYS OF MORGAN CREEK, gives us a couple who are constantly at each other's throats in real life—but their online relationship is another story altogether. And in *Picking Up the Pieces* by Barbara Gale, a world-famous journalist and a former top model risk scandal by following their hearts instead of their heads....

Enjoy them all, and please come back next month for six sensational romances, all from Silhouette Special Edition!

All the best,

Gail Chasan
Senior Editor

Please address questions and book requests to:
Silhouette Reader Service
U.S.: 3010 Walden Ave., P.O. Box 1325, Buffalo, NY 14269
Canadian: P.O. Box 609, Fort Erie, Ont. L2A 5X3

A TYCOON IN TEXAS

CRYSTAL GREEN

Silhouette®

SPECIAL EDITION®

Published by Silhouette Books

America's Publisher of Contemporary Romance

Special thanks and acknowledgment are given to Crystal Green for her contribution to THE FORTUNES OF TEXAS: REUNION series.

To Nancy: Here's to the true love you deserve.

SILHOUETTE BOOKS

ISBN 0-373-24670-6

A TYCOON IN TEXAS

Books by Crystal Green

Silhouette Special Edition

Beloved Bachelor Dad #1374
*The Pregnant Bride #1440
*His Arch Enemy's Daughter #1455
*The Stranger She Married #1498
*There Goes the Bride #1522
Her Montana Millionaire #1574
*The Black Sheep Heir #1587
The Millionaire's Secret Baby #1668
A Tycoon in Texas #1670

*Kane's Crossing

Silhouette Bombshell

The Huntress #28

CRYSTAL GREEN

lives in San Diego, California, where she writes for Silhouette Special Edition, Silhouette Bombshell and Harlequin Blaze. When she isn't penning romances, she loves to read, overanalyze movies, pet her parents' Maltese dog, fence, do yoga and fantasize about being a really good cook.

Whenever possible, Crystal loves to travel. Her favorite souvenirs include journals—the pages reflecting everything from taking tea in London's Leicester Square to wandering the neon-lit streets of Tokyo.

She'd love to hear from her readers at: 8895 Towne Centre Drive, Suite 105-178, San Diego, CA 92122-5542.

And don't forget to visit her Web site at www.crystal-green.com!

Pssst, have you heard?
They're baaack!

Silhouette Special Edition presents three *brand-new* stories about the famous—and infamous!— Fortunes of Texas. Juicy scandals, heart-stopping suspense, love, loss... What else would you expect from the fabulous Fortunes?

Beginning in February 2005, read all about straitlaced CEO Jack Fortune and feisty Gloria Mendoza in RITA® Award-winning author Marie Ferrarella's *Her Good Fortune*, Special Edition #1665....

Then, in March, Gloria's tell-it-like-it-is older sister, Christina Mendoza, finds herself falling hard for boss Derek Rockwell's charming ways, in Crystal Green's *A Tycoon in Texas*, Special Edition #1670....

Finally, watch as youngest sister Sierra tries desperately to ignore her budding feelings for her best friend—and emotional opposite— Alex Calloway, in Stella Bagwell's April installment, *In a Texas Minute*, Special Edition #1677....

The Fortunes of Texas: Reunion—
The price of privilege. The power of family.

Chapter One

No more man temptation.

Christina Mendoza repeated her mantra yet again as she poised a pen over her ink-scrawled legal pad and fixed a cool, all-business gaze on Derek Rockwell.

Her boss. A man she had met only in passing before he had invited her into his office today.

Silence hummed while he perused her report—an analysis based on her observations of Fortune-Rockwell, his company. As sunlight glinted off his dark brown hair, she noticed that his cut—longer on top, shorter on the bottom—was a touch military.

Conservative, demanding.

Hmph. Mr. Rockwell's hair shouldn't be so fascinating to her, Christina thought, waiting for him to finish torturing her with the whole report-card-reading power play. And she shouldn't be thinking about the way his crisp suit accentuated those broad shoulders, either. And, really, while she was at it, the same should go for the slant of those high cheekbones, which were balanced by a strong nose and chin. And as for those brown eyes…

All right. She might as well admit it. No man temptation notwithstanding, she was checking the guy out, just as thoroughly as she had upon briefly meeting him on her first day of work.

Especially his mouth.

While he was still occupied, she took a moment to appreciate his lower lip in particular. It hinted at a possible soft spot his gaze didn't reveal.

Fascinating.

Could he *be* more handsome? Because if there was one thing Christina didn't need, it was a boss who was *muy guapo*. She'd already learned that hormones and office relationships didn't mix.

Learned that quite well.

Besides, she and her sisters had a pact: none of the Mendoza girls—Christina, Gloria nor Sierra—would get involved with men for a year. After Mama had called them back to Red Rock a month ago in order to reconcile the family, the siblings had mended their misunderstandings.

In the flush of reunion, they'd promised each other to put family first, since males had been at the root of all their problems anyway.

And if any of them fell to man temptation before the year was up…oh-oh. It would mean humiliation. Heinous work.

Already, Christina's younger sister, Gloria, had blown her promise to stay away from men. She'd fallen in love with Jack Fortune, the son of the Big Boss—Patrick Fortune.

In fact, Gloria was carrying Jack's child.

Something tugged on Christina's barely used heart. At the age of thirty-two, she was finally going to be an aunt.

Tia Christina. A soft little baby to hold and cuddle. A sign of great love. Of joining with someone who had touched your soul.

She found herself smiling like a romantic dope, but vanquished it just before Derek Rockwell glanced up from the analysis. Never releasing her from eye contact, he sent the papers wafting to his desk.

Christina didn't spare him a blink. In fact, without even looking at the notepad, she scribbled: *Man temptation = bad.*

"Very astute, Ms. Mendoza."

His voice was a low, lazy drawl that couldn't have been cultivated in New York, where he'd been heading up the East Coast branch of Fortune-Rockwell Investments before his former business partner had summoned him here.

That's right. Patrick Fortune was counting on Rockwell to whip the struggling San Antonio offices back into shape, and that's why she'd been hired, too.

If she could manage to stop drooling over her notes long enough to concentrate.

"Thank you, Mr. Rockwell." Her own tone was removed, detached, striking a professional line between her and the boss. Just because he had requested this touch-base meeting didn't mean they had to be office pals. Soon, he'd no doubt go back to working behind a closed door, shutting the rest of the company out. Then she could be relieved of all this hormonal discomfort, all this…*distraction*.

Christina cleared her throat and shifted in her chair as Rockwell ran a slow gaze over her crossed legs, her skirt-covered knees, her Ann Taylor jacket and her upswept hair. Her pulse quickened and followed the trail of his deliberate inspection.

She thought of Gloria again. How she seemed so happy after working things out with Jack. How she'd fulfilled her end of losing the bet by cleaning Christina's and Sierra's houses while dressed in a French maid uniform.

Oh, the price to pay for love.

Christina must have been clenching her teeth—a bad habit—and making a goofy face, because Derek Rockwell was grinning at her. Relaxing back in his chair while a bluebonnet March sky framed him through the window.

His vast walnut desk lent distance, intimidation. Even the sparse decorations—a few exotic musical instruments, such as an Asian-flavored lute and an African-inspired drum—were more statements of taste than personal revelations.

Except for the one picture on his desk. A color-faded photo of a short-haired woman who was hugging two little Maltese dogs.

His mother?

"Now that you've gotten your bearings here, we'll be working closely together," he said, smoothly turning the picture so that it faced away from her. "Since *Patrick* brought you on as our business analyst, I haven't had the chance to talk with you, Christina. To take your measure."

He'd emphasized *Patrick*. A clear sign that just because she'd been hired by the older man, it meant *nada*.

"Mr. Rockwell—" the use of his last name was a statement all in itself "—if you're not pleased with what I've done so far, I'd be happy to discuss it."

"Oh, I like what I see. A degree in business from Texas A&M. Solid references. A good feel for what Fortune-Rockwell needs to get out of the red. I'm just wary. Especially after what the last analyst did to this place."

"So you've got no qualms about Patrick bringing me on?" Might as well get the truth out in the open.

That sidelong grin curved Rockwell's lips, and Christina's heartbeat wavered.

When he leaned forward, his movement fluid and rough all at the same time, she could see why Patrick had told her yesterday that she'd now be working with "my predatory pride and joy."

"I could be slightly put out because Patrick didn't consult me before he hired you. I usually like to have a say in who I work with, *Christina*." As he raised an eyebrow, there was a mildly wicked spark in his gaze. "Or my notable lack of amusement could just be me testing your mettle. It's hard to keep up with me—to be a part of my vision for this company."

Christina bristled at what Derek was no doubt thinking: Patrick was doing the Mendoza family a favor by giving her a job.

"Just in case you're wondering," she said, "I'm not here because of charity. I've earned this opportunity."

Rockwell narrowed his eyes, but settled in to listen.

Encouraged, Christina continued. "While Patrick was getting to know my sisters and me at a reunion, he sensed opportunity. Being a great businessman, he funded Gloria's jewelry business, Love Affair. He had a good feeling about its potential—just like he did about mine."

"So I've heard. Patrick's told me a few things about you and your family, and I listened to him. I trust the man implicitly. He's a great judge of character."

Rockwell stared at her intently, but there was something about the way he did it. Something that made Christina's breath catch. Something that made her want to soften and bat her eyelashes at him.

Oh, brother.

"Then why don't you trust Patrick's judgment in bringing me on?" she asked. "He made a good choice, Mr. Rockwell."

There went that grin again—half carefree flirt, half wolf in designer clothing. "I have to admit that if you impress me half as much as you did him, I'll be appeased."

Blushing, Christina glanced down at her notes. There it went. Shyness mode. It'd never been easy for her to take a compliment.

"However, keep this in mind," Rockwell added. "I'm not real easy to impress."

"Then let's get to work on that now." Christina cleared her throat, sat up straight, chasing the modesty away with her expertise. As usual. "Patrick mentioned that you want to rubber-stamp my new ideas."

"Wait." He made a nonchalant show of loosening his tie. "We'll get to your spiel in a second. I kind of like to be comfortable with my co-workers before talking numbers."

Unable to control her inner fantasy machine, Christina thought, *Comfortable, you say? Well, then let me undo my own figurative tie and we'll go from there.*

Oooo. Bad. Very, very bad. Office relationships meant big trouble, whether you asked for them or not.

Awful, naughty thoughts.

He continued, clearly unaware of her *chica*-in-heat struggles.

"You grew up around San Antonio?" he asked.

Could she relax a little? Giving him a tiny bit of information wouldn't be an impropriety. And besides, Patrick, a family friend, could give Rockwell all the gossip he wanted. What would be the harm in some chatting?

Still, she fidgeted in her seat. "Yes, I did. My family's home is in Red Rock. My parents live just down the road from the Double Crown Ranch, which belongs to Patrick's brother, Ryan."

"I'd like to see it someday. Patrick tells me you had to quit your job in California to come back home. That must've been tough."

Okay, this she didn't want to talk about. How, years ago, she and Gloria had experienced a falling-out because of a former co-worker. How sister had betrayed sister. How Sierra, the baby of their family, had been torn between Gloria and Christina. Their petty arguments. Their bickering.

Things had gotten so uncomfortable that Christina had eventually moved to Los Angeles, fleeing her family in a flurry of shame and distrust. Gloria had moved to Denver.

Sierra had stayed home, too preoccupied with everyone else's lives to really have one of her own.

Even now, guilt consumed Christina. It'd taken a panicked—yet false—phone call from Mama to bring her back to Red Rock.

Papa has chest pains, she'd said. *Please come to see him.*

Gloria had gotten the same call, but it was only after Mama had locked all three of the sisters into a room to hash out their problems that they'd learned their orchestrating matriarch had been exaggerating about Papa's sickness.

An anxiety attack. That's what it was.

But, in all honesty, Christina's own heart had always been in Red Rock. She'd just needed a good excuse to return to it.

She doodled the loving shape on her note pad. "It wasn't so hard to come back here at all."

A beat of silence separated the conversation into two halves: the subject of Red Rock and the expectation that Christina would ask about *his* personal life, in return.

When she didn't pursue the opening, Derek took the hint.

Damn, she was a cold one. He'd even gotten that feeling during their first how-do-you-do last month, before he'd buried himself in work and the soothing pattern of forgetfulness.

But, when all was said and done, he wouldn't have told her squat even if she'd asked.

Sure, he would've given her the usual platitudes: deceased mother and father, de facto son of the heart to Patrick Fortune, who'd plucked Derek from college and mentored him straight into an ultrasuccessful business career.

Hell, with a bit of small talk, Christina Mendoza might even be an easier conquest than she appeared to be. He'd seen it happen before.

But…nah. She was emanating those stay-away vibes, and he could respect that. Business was more important than his enjoyment of a good time anyway. It was hard to get good employees, yet not so hard to snag one-night stands.

He held back a smile. *Women.* He loved the silhouettes of their bodies, the purr of their voices, the softness of their curves.

And Ms. Christina Mendoza was hiding it all, with her stoic, brown linen suit. The gold of her studded earrings and simple necklace. The ivory, sun-shaped clip that captured her cocoa-brown hair.

But her demure chignon revealed something that must've been an oversight. A sexy whisper of what was surely underneath all that quiet wrapping…

A graceful, slender neck.

In a flash of pure lust, Derek could imagine the taste of her pulse, her rosy skin, as he dragged his mouth up her throat. He would kiss his way up to her jaw, over her delicate cheekbones, to the tilt of her hazel eyes.

In response, those long, toned legs of hers would wrap around his body, allowing her to lean back— maybe even over the expanse of his office desk— then to press into the ever-awakening beat of his arousal.

Derek's pants had gotten pretty tight, just thinking about what *wouldn't* happen with his employee. He changed position in his stuffed leather chair, hoping to tuck away his hunger and get on with business.

His movement attracted her attention away from that notepad of hers.

You'd think she'd written out the solution to world peace from the way she stared at those scribblings, he thought.

Derek opened his mouth to make more conversation, to relax her—or was it to relax him? To let her know that she could count on him to keep to his "boss" role—or was he only convincing himself?

But that's when he spied Jack Fortune through the office window, strolling past the assistant's desk and toward the door. Great.

With his black hair and tall frame, Jack didn't exactly cry out, "Patrick's son!" Oddly enough, his dad was a redhead, and no one in the family could explain where the coloring had come from.

"Hope I'm in time to hear Ms. Mendoza reveal her big new plans for Fortune-Rockwell," Jack said, standing by Christina's chair and extending his hand in greeting.

Not surprisingly, Christina perked up. Jack was almost a part of her family, what with him getting one of the Mendoza sisters pregnant.

Careless.

She shook Jack's hand. "Congratulations on taking over Patrick's holdings," she said. "And on my little niece or nephew."

"Thank you. I guess you deserve kudos yourself."

Christina smiled. "Why is that?"

"You managed to get Gloria to clean your house. A masterstroke of genius."

"Well, it wasn't as incredible as your successes with Fortune, TX, Limited, Jack. I'm eager to hear what you have in store for Fortune-Rockwell Investments, too."

Derek arranged his features into a neutral mask. It wasn't smart to let Jack see how much it rankled that Patrick had recently transferred all his business holdings to his son. Derek and Patrick had been a great team, so why had his mentor gone into semi-retirement and given Jack control?

True, Derek and Jack worked well together, too, even with the tension between them. But, still, Derek already missed strategizing with his surrogate father on a daily basis.

Jack folded his lean body onto the leather couch, still talking to Christina. "We're hoping to see better results with you, Christina. You know about the damage this branch sustained from the last business analyst."

"I know he recommended massive layoffs," Christina said, reciting her knowledge as if she were briefing the Pentagon. "And even though his ideas increased bottom-line profits for the short term, they resulted in poor employee morale. You fired the analyst after the layoffs backfired."

"Someone's up on current events," Jack said.

Hey, Fortune-Rockwell was *Derek's* baby. So why the hell was Jack doing all the talking?

Standing, Derek moved to the front of his desk,

right in front of Christina. He leaned against it, crossing his arms over his chest.

"We've got the layoffs *and* two new bosses breathing down the employees' necks," he said, "and that makes matters even worse."

Efficiently, Christina dug into a briefcase resting near her fashionable, yet practical white-and-brown pumps, then produced two bound reports. She rose to her feet, presenting Derek with one and Jack with the other.

"Don't worry. You hired me to come up with ways to increase employee productivity, and that's what I'll do." She stood in the center of the room, a hand braced on one hip, cocky as you please. "These are some statistics and research for you to look over before we go any further."

Damn, she had such great legs. Long, trim…

The sound of Jack flipping open his report redirected Derek's wandering focus.

But that didn't keep him from casting one last glance at her gorgeous figure before devoting himself to the numbers.

The cover read, "How to Tell the Employees They're Important: Providing Personal Growth Opportunities to Improve Morale."

Perfect. Touchy-feely, la-di-da solutions to a serious problem.

She was already launching into her pitch. "As you can see from the graphs, tables and charts, many studies show that when employees have the perception that the corporation cares, they want to do well for the company. Their sense of loyalty increases. Many even look forward to coming to work. I'd like to explore ways to get our employees into the company spirit again, whether it's through personal growth classes, recreation options or even day care for families."

Derek was just about to ask how much money this would cost when Jack spoke up.

"Classes. I like that. The employees would see right off the bat that we're here to make some positive changes. Best of all, their new skills might even transfer over to their jobs in some way. Christina, if you concentrate on that aspect first, how soon can you have a presentation ready?"

What? Derek shot a curious glance over to his new partner. No questions? No reservations?

"Give me a week," she said, all guns blazing.

Suddenly, the woman who seemed covered by brown linen and a reserved shield was absolutely glowing. Derek's belly went silly with the aphrodisiac of her spirit.

Work. Concentrate on work, you dog.

"Classes," he said, really needing to hear how this was going to help turn their investment firm around.

"Yes, classes," said a booming voice from the office entrance. "Good idea."

They all looked at Patrick Fortune, who was leaning against the door frame, dressed to the nines in spit-polished Italian loafers and a pin-striped suit.

The older man, whose red hair was just beginning to show shimmers of white, didn't look—or act—his seventy years. The only sign of advancing age, besides a few wrinkles, were the glasses he wore over those sparkling blue eyes.

Derek couldn't help smiling. "About time you reported to work."

"Can't keep him away," muttered Jack with a touch of fondness.

Christina had already retrieved another report from her briefcase and was bringing it to the elder man. "This is old hat for you, Patrick. I recited most of these statistics to you at the party."

Oh, so, it was *Patrick?*

"Thank you, my dear," the magnate said, accepting the material.

With a doting smile, Christina nodded. Derek couldn't help thinking that her switch from business warrior to beaming woman was sort of cute. Well, real cute, actually.

But *cute* wasn't a very good description for Christina Mendoza. Cute was for cheerleaders who never grew up. No, this woman was what you'd call *willowy*. Sexy. Hot.

A knockout just waiting to rip off her schoolteacher costume at the right moment.

Yeah, thought Derek. And if she needed any help taking down her hair…

Patrick was staring at him, picking up on Derek's playboy instincts, no doubt.

Without thinking, Derek straightened his tie. "Ms. Mendoza plans to show us some definitive plans next week."

"Next week?"

Patrick steepled his fingers together, going into deep-thinking mode. Brilliant things came out of this posture. Clever ideas for new mergers, diabolical budget adjustments, genius proposals.

"Dad," Jack said, "this sure doesn't look like retirement to me."

"Retirement?" Derek laughed. "The word isn't in the man's vocabulary, Jack."

"I know." The other man shrugged. "You'd like him to be your business partner forever, but—"

"But I'm lucky enough to have you as Tweedledum to my Tweedledee now."

Derek caught Christina's curious gaze as she took in the tension.

Out of the corner of his eye, he saw Jack bristle, caught with his emotional pants down, too.

"Gentlemen." Patrick was used to these mild flare-ups between them. "You must have realized something already."

See? Incoming brilliant idea.

"A week is a short time to expect Christina to put together a strong presentation," Patrick said.

She lifted a finger. "No problem. I can do it."

"Why make yourself work night and day when it could be so much easier?" Patrick sauntered away from the door, toward Derek. "It'd be wise, I believe, to give you a crack team who knows every nuance of Fortune-Rockwell philosophy. I've got some employees in mind to lend you support."

When Christina started to protest, Derek interrupted. "Don't be a Lone Ranger. Having someone who knows Fortune-Rockwell inside and out would be a great asset to you."

Maybe he could even handpick that person so they could report back to him about what their new analyst was preparing. He was hands-on, all right, but still a delegator.

Patrick came to stand by Derek, lifting a hand up to rest it on his protégé's shoulder. "I'm glad you agree, Derek. How about working with Christina on this? You could handle the financial side of our campaign to promote morale, and she could be the creative force."

Damn. He should've seen that one coming.

But, naturally, he'd been a little distracted by long legs and shining hair.

Good God, he didn't have time to do her job, too. How could he get out of this?

As Jack rose from the couch, he chuckled. "I look forward to seeing your presentation next week, Christina."

Then he jerked his chin at Derek, highly entertained. "And Derek."

Right, Derek thought as he merely nodded his head, tracking Jack as he left the room. *Thanks for dumping this on me.*

Jack had obviously sensed that his new partner wouldn't have an easy time accepting Christina's ideas. It happened all the time, with them on opposite sides. Then again, that's why they balanced each other, made for a decent team.

It was hard to admit, but there was some idiot part of Derek that wanted to impress Jack, wanted to still make Patrick proud, as well.

Ridiculous. A thirty-five-year-old shouldn't need to win over big brother and father figures.

Patrick's loud voice brought Derek back to the moment.

"You two have a lot of work to be done," he said, clapping his hands and rubbing them together. "I suppose you should get started. Christina, is there anything I can do to help you?"

"No, I've got everything I need in my office."

As Christina moved to her briefcase, Patrick winked at Derek. Then, with a spring in his step, he took off.

"Thanks," muttered Derek so only Patrick could hear.

Without looking back, his associate lifted a hand and left Christina and Derek alone, silence hanging in the office like limp streamers after the party had ended.

Classes. Recreation. Day care.

The softer side of Cutthroat Rockwell was about to be tested.

He found Christina staring at him, a wary look in her intelligent eyes as she lifted the briefcase to her side.

Something in his chest clenched, though he couldn't say what it was.

Didn't matter anyway.

Shrugging out of his jacket, Derek smiled at his new project team member.

"So what do you say we get down to running some numbers?" he asked, already wondering if he could trick Jack into taking his place.

Without waiting for her response, he retreated to the most comfortable place in the world.

Behind his desk.

Chapter Two

Bright and early the next morning, after having laid the groundwork for Christina's changes yesterday, Derek greeted his assistant, Dora. She'd seemed more downbeat than usual, her extralank black hair only emphasizing the perception.

"What's ailing you?" he asked after entering his lobby. Her frown made him want to make her smile again. "You have a cold? Were you out of orange juice this a.m.? Or maybe Tom Cruise is getting married again?"

He gestured to the toothy movie-star pictures that decorated her desk like minibillboards for proper hygienic care. Somehow, she managed to keep her workstation professional without having it resemble a shrine, so in the short time he'd been in San Antonio, he hadn't asked her to clear the area.

Besides, the morale around the offices really did stink, and he wasn't about to nitpick when things were at their lowest. He knew how to choose his battles.

Long ago, with the man he'd called Sir, Derek had learned how to keep his peace or sacrifice it each night over dinner. Every confrontation with Sir had been Armageddon, a father-son apocalypse.

Dora huffed out a sigh. "Everyone's a little bummed, actually. It's the analyst."

"Christina Mendoza?" Good God, she was already on everyone's nerves?

"Yeah. We're all wondering what she has up her sleeve. More layoffs?"

Tilting her head, Dora widened her eyes, trying to wheedle information out of him since it was no secret that he was now working closely with the analyst.

Not as closely as his libido would like, but that was another issue.

"No more layoffs," he said, noting that he'd need to send out a memo pronto, assuring the staff that they weren't going to be terminated. "We're functioning at bare bones already. Don't worry about that, Dora."

She exhaled. "Oh, thank goodness. I thought all those papers she dumped on your desk this morning were bad news."

Papers, huh?

It wasn't until he walked into his office that he realized what Dora had meant by papers.

As in a mound of them.

Catalogs about sewing classes, personal investment courses, literature circles.

"Dora," he said into his intercom, "could you please ask the human dump truck to come into my office?"

As he waited for Christina, he removed the junk from his desktop and settled in for a long day.

Not that he had anywhere to go other than Fortune-Rockwell. In New York, he would've been in a limo at six o'clock, off to an event by seven, then in some gorgeous woman's bed by ten. However, lately, he'd been too busy for a social life, but he'd get right to work on that.

Just as soon as he put these offices back where they belonged.

Ten minutes later, Christina appeared, holding another bound report and dressed in a nondescript sand-colored ensemble, her hair pulled back by a turquoise clip. It was the only stylish thing about her wardrobe.

Even so, he could catch a stunning glimpse of hidden beauty.

"Sit down, Christina," he said, his gut fisting in a repeat of fruitless lust.

It was something he'd just have to get used to until he had time for wining and dining again.

"Thank you." She moved to occupy the chair in

front of his desk, but found that it was buried under the Mount Everest of her catalogs.

She glanced up at him. "A subtle hint?"

"I like you. You catch on quickly."

"Yes, I do. In any case, Mr. Rockwell, I wanted you to see some of the classes that are available. I highlighted the ones that might appeal the most."

"I don't have time for leisurely afternoons spent thumbing through catalogs."

She waited a beat, gauging him, then shook her head. "I could tell you weren't into this from the get-go. You aren't entirely convinced that my ideas are the best way to bring about change. You're a numbers guy, and that's how you're used to operating. It's how you cultivated your wealth."

"Again, you've done your homework."

"The annual reports told me a lot." A flush had suffused her cheeks, bringing out the colors of her desert-at-sunrise eyes. "But, with this branch of Fortune-Rockwell, you're dealing with people problems. And they directly affect your beloved numbers."

Yeah, yeah. He knew. And, as Patrick had told him time and again, Derek was just too stubborn to admit it.

Still…basket-weaving classes?

She'd stepped forward, offering the covered report she'd been holding. "Here. I've summarized the possibilities. Today, I'd like to put together a survey so I can see what the employees would like to learn. Foreign languages, relaxing crafts, life skills?"

He tapped the report against his desk. "Did you sleep at all last night?"

"I…" She swallowed, paused. "I wanted to be up to speed."

It was almost as if she didn't want to lead him anywhere near her bedroom, her mattress, her off-hours even in conversation.

Damn, why was it that the one woman who had no interest in him tickled his fancy?

The attraction didn't make sense at all, not when she was the opposite of his usual type. Normally, Derek enjoyed the company of what Patrick called Women Lite.

"Just like watered-down beer," the old man had always said. "Less filling, with half the intelligence."

Derek usually blew off his partner's observations, knowing how uncomfortably true they were. But, still, he didn't want relationships any other way.

No commitment, no worry. That was his philosophy.

Derek stood, went to the opposite chair, removed the catalogs and ushered her into the seat with an opened palm. As she sat down, a sweet, erotic scent wafted past him.

Exotic leaves, crushed to a mist of herbal smoke.

He imagined tasting the tang of it on her skin, allowing it to be absorbed into him.

But Derek didn't do romance that way. He kept women from getting under his skin. At all costs.

"Mr. Rockwell?"

He glanced at Christina, finding her watching him

with the same probing questions she'd no doubt been mulling over yesterday, after he'd exchanged words with Jack.

Don't ask me if everything's okay, he thought. You already have the right idea by keeping it all business.

A cheery voice piped over his thoughts.

"Are we starting yet?"

Derek turned to find a petite blonde garbed in a tiny red skirt with a white sleeveless blouse. Her curly hair gave her the air of a Shirley Temple doll, dimples and all.

Christina laid eyes on her, too, and the microskirt set her eyebrows to winging.

"Hi," the girl chirped, extending a hand to him. "I'm Twyla, one of your team members."

"You are?" asked Christina.

Derek made short work of shaking the young woman's hand. Already, his Lite tracking system had alerted the male radar.

Concentrating hard on Christina's comparatively grandmother-like clothing, he hoped the blah colors would be enough to get him back on track.

And…yes. Success. But maybe it wasn't the clothing that had done the trick.

Maybe it was Christina herself, with those all-knowing eyes, the genteel lines of her posture.

Her class.

Suddenly, staying on this project sounded pretty good to him.

As Twyla attacked Christina's hand in greeting, Derek cleared his head and motioned to the couch. "How long have you been working for Fortune-Rockwell?"

"Oh, a few years, right out of college. Jack Fortune assigned me to your project this morning."

"That was decent of him." Derek's fist clenched, just itching to do some throttling. So Jack had sent his own spy, had he? "I've asked two other employees to join our team, too, so we'll wait for them before we start."

"Oops." Twyla had dropped her pen on the floor as she made her way to the couch.

Bending over to pick it up, she flashed a load of cleavage in Derek's direction, then lifted her head to see if he was looking.

God, he was a guy—one who'd been stuck in the office for too damned long. Of course he was looking.

But Derek didn't date his employees. It was a good way to get into big trouble.

When he glanced back at Christina, he realized how uninterested he was in this particular brand of Lite anyway.

He only wished she wasn't looking at him as if he were a scum-guzzling slug of humanity.

As nightfall darkened Christina's office, she heard Twyla yawn from a love seat that had decorated every office she'd had since graduating from business school.

All her furnishings were old and sentimental, as a matter of fact: Mexican artwork featuring different moods of the sun, ironwork sculptures, baskets filled with sage. She'd spent so much time in her offices that she'd decorated them to be homes away from home.

"I'll be here for a while yet," she said. "Why don't you call it a day, Twyla?"

Instantly, the girl was on her feet. "Are you sure? Because I can stay."

"No, really. You've been very helpful." And, surprisingly, Christina meant it. She'd had her doubts at first, with that dental floss miniskirt and all, but Twyla was a devoted worker. "Really. Go."

"Okay. Then I'll see you tomorrow."

And in two shakes of a lamb's tail, she was gone, leaving Christina with an endless To-Do list.

But she didn't mind so much. Work was her life.

It saved her from thinking about the silence of the condo she'd recently purchased here in town. The echoing drip of a faucet that someday needed fixing. The sound of the radio playing salsa music to keep her company.

As long as she watched her step here at Fortune-Rockwell, she'd have work to keep her content. In all honesty, she couldn't afford another repeat of what had happened years ago at Macrizon: the heartbreak of having a boss turn on her. The shock of finding out that her fellow employees were no better.

Christina's fingers slackened over her keyboard.

Bosses.

She was trying so hard to stay in line where Derek Rockwell was concerned. Sure, she'd caught him giving her the once-over a time or two, but that was normal behavior for men in power. Back at Macrizon, her superior, William Dugan, had given her plenty of attention.

And look what that had gotten her.

A tail-between-the-legs trip to California, where she'd deserted her family—her true, constant friends.

Well, that wasn't going to happen this time. Not with Rockwell.

Even if she wanted to jump his bones every time she was alone with him.

"How do you function without any shut-eye?"

She glanced up to find him filling her doorway.

With his shirt sleeves rolled up to reveal muscled forearms, and with his tie and collar loosened, he still seemed perfectly put together. Structured and in control.

But oddly enough, as he rested his hands on the door's steel frame, he reminded Christina of a man calmly trying to keep the building from falling down around him.

The image connected him to her, made him seem a little more human and a little less dangerous.

Rolling her head, she worked a few cricks out of her neck. Then she stretched, trying to disguise how much he effected her.

"I'm one of those lucky people, I suppose," she said. "I can live on three hours of sleep."

"I don't know." He let go of the frame and wandered farther into her office. "Beds are one of the joys of life."

An attempted response stuck in her throat.

"Sorry." He laughed, ran a hand over his short, neat hair. "I didn't mean to make you uncomfortable."

She wanted to tell him that, years ago, he wouldn't have. That it had taken one bad experience to put her on edge forever.

He continued, having stopped in his tracks at her silence.

"How long will you be here?" he asked.

"Let's see." Exhaling, she checked the amethyst-crystal clock on her desk. "Eternity?"

Grinning—and how lethal it was—he jerked a thumb toward the door. "Let's grab something to eat at that café on the corner. Nothing untoward in my intentions, okay? I'm hungry, and I'm sure you are, too."

She thought about all her problems at Macrizon. The worst of them had started when she'd had an innocent drink with William Dugan, then a business dinner. By the time he'd invited her on a trip to service a client, she'd trusted him. And that's when he'd pounced, revealing that he'd booked only one hotel room.

With only one bed.

Derek's voice cut in. "The café's got great pasta dishes. You like Italian?"

Oh, did she ever. In fact, she liked food, period. And her stomach had grumbled about twenty-two times over the last half hour…

"A quick bite to eat?" she said. "And can I run a few ideas past you?"

"Yes and yes. We'll be back in a flash, because I know how attached you are to your office chair."

"Ha-ha." She cut herself off from making a smart remark, but she was smiling all the same.

Minutes later, they were riding the elevator down in almost palpable tension, then strolling to the corner café.

It was a brightly lit place, with yellow awnings and a fern-strewn courtyard. The cooling night breeze was still nice enough for outdoor dining so, after ordering, they settled themselves at a white metal table where they could enjoy the spring weather.

See, she thought, sitting across from him and perking up her good old healthy salad with a splash of vinegar, then oil. This wasn't so compromising.

No fodder for the corporate rumor mill.

As she contemplated her greens, dying for something more fattening, Rockwell dug into his lasagna. She couldn't help watching.

Ummm. Layers of mozzarella with a white, creamy sauce. If she'd ordered it, she'd be jogging for hours at the crack of dawn just to work off the calories.

Mouth swimming with flavor-desperate drool, she realized that Rockwell had caught her staring.

His brown eyes gleamed. "Want some?"

"No, no," she said, recovering, then depositing a leaf of romaine lettuce into her mouth.

"Lasagna hits the spot." He continued demolishing his food. "Since I arrived in town, I've made a habit of eating here every day. Usually, though, I order up to the office."

Was he another version of her? A workaholic?

"I try to stay healthy," she said. "But I…"

Okay, time to shut up. He didn't want to know how she secretly lusted after potato chips, buttered popcorn, raw chocolate-chip cookie dough straight from the fridge.

"Not a trace of junk food junkie in you?" he asked, taking a swig from a glass of bottled water. He set the beverage down. "With your physique, you can afford to splurge now and then."

There it went again—the blushing. "I like salads. Really. And jogging. And I'm addicted to yoga."

As well as anything covered in chocolate.

"I can tell." He held up his hands. "Not that I mean to compliment you or anything. I know you don't like that."

She stopped, the fork halfway to her mouth. Sure she enjoyed the praise. Especially from Rockwell.

Not that she liked liking it.

Her blush intensified. Dang it. "I just… I don't know. I just don't know you very well, I suppose. And I'm used to keeping business as business." She shoved more lettuce into her old talking hole.

"That's a good philosophy."

"Mmm." Yup, that was her witty rejoinder. She was too busy eating and trying to pretend her salad was lasagna to offer anything more.

"But it can get kind of lonely thinking that way."

Suddenly, she really couldn't taste the food.

Neither of them moved for a second, and then they both went back to eating. Dean Martin, bless his heart, made up for the stilted conversation with his winking rendition of "That's Amore."

Saved by the good-natured lyrics, they ate and ate, pausing every once in a while to chat about Fortune-Rockwell, finding their footing in business once again.

By the time they'd cleared their plates, Christina was relaxed.

Discovering your groove with a new co-worker always took some time, she thought. They'd just needed to get over the initial testing of personal boundaries.

As they strolled onto the sidewalk, she breathed in the night air—crisp and laced with garlic from the café's food.

She stopped walking. Then he did, too.

"I really needed that, Mr. Rockwell," she said, grinning. "Thanks for dragging me outside."

With cautious steps, he backtracked to where she was standing, coming to tower over her. A shadow blanketing her body, warming it.

"Glad to help."

God, she couldn't swallow.

Could he actually be stealing the strength from her? Drawing it out just by standing so close? Her body felt weaker with each shortened breath. Sapped by his nearness.

She focused on the first thing that caught her attention—the tiny, upturned wrinkle of his collar.

Funny, she thought, half in a daze. He's not so impossibly structured after all.

"You're…" Gathering all her energy back from him, she pointed at his collar. "…falling apart."

He cocked an eyebrow, then glanced down. With care, he smoothed out the material.

She could imagine his closets, his drawers, filled with starched, regimented clothing.

Then, as if she'd never even pointed out an imperfection in him, he started walking away.

"We've got a lot of work to do, Ms. Mendoza. You coming?"

Of course, she thought, knowing business was the only way to forget all the wrinkles between them.

Especially the one in her judgment.

Patrick Fortune had tried to seem casual as he sauntered by the café for the third time. With every pass, he'd whispered into the cell phone that was poised next to his ear.

"They're still talking," he said, trying to stifle his voice level.

Lacey, his lovely wife, always told him that he could bring down all of his Fortune high-rise buildings with merely his voice. But it was hard to keep quiet when one had so much to say.

On the other end of the line, Maria Mendoza spoke up. "Now what are they doing?"

Patrick had made it around the corner without Christina or Derek spying him. "Still talking. But there's a lot of eating going on, also. I was hoping they'd be so enthralled with each other that the food would go cold."

The sound of clicking knitting needles told Patrick that Christina's mother and her good friend and cousin, Rosita Perez, were drinking tea and making scarves in the kitchen. They had him on speakerphone—the better to plot by, my dear.

Rosita offered her opinion. "It was a rough start with Jack and Gloria, also. Let's remember how hard those two were to manage."

"Who can forget?" asked Maria. "It is not easy being a schemer."

Patrick had crept toward the café again, adjusting his glasses and peeking around the brick wall into the courtyard. He was rewarded with a view of the couple—or not-a-couple—still stuffing food into their mouths.

Matchmaking Project, The Sequel: Derek and Christina.

A man who wasn't sure how to love and, in Patrick's opinion, needed to be taught how to *truly* enjoy life.

An extremely smart woman who had a strong will and an innocent heart.

The two were made for each other and, soon, they'd know it.

Patrick had walked to safety yet another time. "I thought for certain Derek would move a little quicker here. You should've seen the way he was looking at Christina yesterday."

Rosita spoke up. "It's probably all Christina's fault. If it were not for that silly bet the girls have going, this would be much easier. Oh, the poor brainy child. She just does not have such good luck with men."

"Qué lastima." Maria sighed. "What a shame she cannot find the joy Gloria has. And I feel for my Sierra, too! I only wish all my daughters could be happy."

"They will be," Patrick said, one hundred and ten percent certain of it. "I've engineered so many successful mergers in my time, that I can close a deal in my sleep. I'm banking on sealing this one, as well."

"Hallelujah!" both women said together.

In the background, Patrick heard Maria's husband, Jose, mutter, *"Loco.* All of you."

"Don't you have a restaurant to run?" Maria said to him. Then, to Patrick, "He thinks I dwell too much on the girls' problems."

Rosita made an argumentative sound. "Oh, no. A mother can never think about her children too much. True, you have many to concern yourself with…"

Yes, Patrick thought, spurred by the prospect of giving a guiding hand to each Mendoza child in turn. Gloria, Christina, then Sierra, and Jorge, and Roberto. What good was being rich unless you could spread around the wealth and happiness?

"Don't worry about it, Maria," he said. "I'm finding that semiretirement has given me some extra time to fill. I'll be around for each of your little darlings in turn."

"Bless you, Patrick."

The sound of two women blowing him kisses traveled over the airwaves, and he shrugged modestly.

It was nice to be appreciated.

"Now," he said, "we have to admit that their going out to eat together is a very positive sign. And since I've forced proximity by requesting that Derek work with Christina, I've got a good feeling about this."

"Optimist." That was Maria.

"Don't lose heart, here." At that point, he'd heard the sound of people exiting the café, so he ducked behind a building's corner. "We just have to take this—their first meeting—to the next logical step."

"A barbecue!" Maria said.

It was the Mendoza solution for everything.

"When?" he asked.

"This weekend."

"I'll invite Derek."

"I'll take care of getting the girls here."

Patrick bit his lip as the people walked by him. Derek and Christina.

He squinted shut his eyes, hoping to high heaven they wouldn't see him.

They didn't. But they did stop about fifteen yards down the way.

"I'll report back later," Patrick whispered into his phone, then folded it into the off position.

As he peeked around the corner, he saw his protégé hovering over Christina.

There you go, kid. If there's one woman who's worth all your playboy charm, Christina is it.

As long as Derek treated her well, Patrick amended. And he'd damn well be around to make sure it happened.

With that, the old pot stirrer merged back into the night, already applauding the progress of The Sequel.

Chapter Three

While Christina sipped merlot from a wineglass, the Saturday sunshine bathed her body. She was reclining in a wooden chair on the Mendozas' back patio, enjoying one of the many family barbecues she'd missed during her absence.

A few neighborhood children ran around the spacious lawn, their yelps of "Tag, you're it!" mingling with the spicy aroma of *carne asada*, Jose Mendoza's signature beef specialty. It's what his restaurant, Red, was best known for—that, and the flavorful margaritas.

One of the children, five-year-old Sancho from down the road, took a dive in the grass, and before

Christina could rise from her seat to go to him, another guest beat her to it.

The indomitable Ryan Fortune, muscular and tanned from years of ranch work, sprang from his chair at an umbrella-shrouded table. He'd been sitting with his striking wife Lily, Patrick's elegant mate Lacey and Jack Fortune, as well as Rosita and Ruben Perez. All of them had been laughing over some sort of shared joke.

Three other tables of neighbors applauded Ryan's safety efforts as he winged Sancho up from the ground and persuaded the dust-bitten child not to cry.

Why wasn't she laughing and clapping with everyone else instead of sitting here alone?

Staring into the deep red of her wine, Christina knew the exact reason. She was too immersed in work, even though she'd earned rest after a harried week blurred by late nights and brainstorming sessions.

Although she and Derek had gone to the café that one night, they'd been too busy to do it again, with her concentrating on this project and him returning to all his other responsibilities. Besides, they were always surrounded by the other three people on their team, affording no chances for breaks or personal chats. All of them had been working like maniacs these past few days to prep for the presentation.

Which was due Monday.

Yet they were ready. Christina had told this to Rockwell an hour ago, when he'd called to summon her to the office today.

"What's wrong?" she'd asked. "I thought we covered all the bases."

"Not all. I came up with something new. I need to discuss it with you, then enlist your help in adjusting the presentation materials to reflect my idea."

Even though, as a perfectionist, she was too willing to believe something was missing in her finished products, there was no way she would ditch a family gathering for something that could be taken care of tonight.

"You're suddenly into the notion of these classes now," she'd said. "Aren't you?"

He'd paused, the silence long and intimidating. Not that she cared.

"Christina…" His voice held a warning.

She'd smiled then.

"I can come in after my family barbecue."

He'd started to protest, but she'd shut off her cell phone, unwilling to be persuaded. At the same time, she'd felt somewhat victorious, knowing she'd won him to her side, even a little.

Unfortunately, he'd gone on to call the Mendoza residence and Jack's cell, but Christina had refused to talk to him anymore. He could take her help later tonight or leave it.

Family needed to be more important than anything else: work, herself…men.

Rockwell.

Darn this attraction she felt growing every day.

She couldn't help noticing the details: How their

office chairs would subtly wheel closer to each other. How the wrinkle in his collar never seemed to go away with each change of shirt. How Twyla would covertly stare at him just as much as Christina probably did.

Not that she should be worrying about such a thing. Let Twyla have him. It'd be a load off Christina's mind.

Even if she did go home at night to lie between the cool sheets of her bed, fantasizing about his hands covering her skin, warming places that had gone untouched for too long.

Ay. Fantasies about the boss.

No wonder she was such a wreck. She hadn't been this chemically attracted to, this shaken up over, a man for…

Well, for ages.

As a friendly cheer sounded from Ryan's table, Christina glanced up, finding that the darkly handsome older man had brought little Sancho back with him to rest on his lap. The child was grinning from ear to ear, even though there was a patch of grass hanging from his chin.

When a gentle, soft hand settled on Christina's shoulder, she looked up to find her mama.

"Once again, you are thinking too much," Maria Mendoza said.

"Mama, I'm going cold turkey, so have mercy. I actually refused to go into work to be here." Christina rose from her seat, unable to sit still. The irony. "You need help serving?"

"Gloria and Sierra are taking care of the kitchen. Sit back down."

A slight breeze tweaked Mama's dark, gray-glinted hair. She was wearing a sundress, which outlined her curvy figure to full advantage. Like her daughters, she had the same rosy, tanned skin.

With a rush of appreciation, Christina smiled, grateful that she'd been summoned back here so she could absorb the beauty of her mama again.

"There's no rest for the wicked," Christina said, patting her mother's cheek.

As she started walking toward the kitchen to help her sisters anyway, Mama's voice rang out.

"Christina Maria Mendoza, you come back here."

Ooo, the middle-name game. Trouble.

Like a good daughter, Christina returned, holding back a laugh.

Maria took Christina's hand in hers, made eye contact with Rosita Perez, and motioned her distant cousin over. "You haven't told me or Rosita about your life lately. Your job."

"Oh, you know, same old grind."

Rosita, a short, pleasantly plump woman who had the coolest hair—dark with a white streak darting down one side—reminded Christina of a fairy godmother. A Disney *Sleeping Beauty* sort, with her hair in a bun and a magic-wand sparkle about her.

Mama took her friend's hand, as well. "Tell Rosita all about Fortune-Rockwell since she hasn't heard the details yet."

"Yes," said the tiny woman, "I want to know everything. What is your office like? What sort of people do you work with?"

Rockwell. Heat shot through Christina like a blaze from a flare gun.

Someone help me, she thought.

"They're normal working people," she said, shrugging. "Just a bunch of type A's who shuffle papers and stare at computer screens until their eyes cross."

"Is Jack treating you well?" Mama asked.

"Very."

"How about your other boss," Rosita added. "I cannot remember his name…"

"Rockhard." Mama nodded with finality, because if Mama said it, that's how it was.

Christina couldn't help laughing. "This is an investment firm, Mama. A man with a name like Rockhard needs to make his way to a soap opera."

"Oh." Her mother lightly slapped her forehead with an opened palm. "Then what is his name?"

Was it Christina's imagination, or were Rosita and Mama just a little too interested in Mr. Rockhard?

"Rockwell," she answered. "Derek Rockwell."

Rosita was nodding. "Yes, he is the one. We invited him to our fiesta, but he turned us down."

For her part, Mama was waving hello toward the adobe-style house, where Patrick Fortune was emerging.

"Isn't that right, Patrick?" she yelled. "Your partner was too good for our company."

With hugs and kisses, Patrick joined their circle, adjusting his glasses. He was as casually dressed as the rest of them, garbed in a blue polo shirt and lightweight slacks.

"Quite the contrary," he said, looking none too pleased that his protégé wasn't taking some time off today. "Derek's buried at the office, he tells me."

While Patrick took Christina in his paternal embrace, she felt guilty for being here while Rockwell was working. But she took comfort from Patrick's smell: black licorice and aftershave.

Holding her away from him, Patrick inspected her. "You look tired. Derek tells me you don't sleep enough."

Mama and Rosita both clucked their tongues.

"But he did say you two had dinner the other night," Patrick added, exchanging a meaningful glance with Mama and Rosita.

Just as Christina was starting to get an odd feeling about all these Rockhard comments and questions, her brother Jorge emerged out of the back door and onto the patio.

All the neighbor women, married or not, stopped talking and gave him the once-over.

Her brother. The guy with a daredevil swagger and dark hair tied back into a low ponytail. God's gift to females.

"Here I am to rescue you, Christina." He wrapped

an arm around her shoulders and maneuvered her toward the kitchen entrance. "Sierra assigned me this daunting task."

Christina steadied her wineglass, which had sloshed a bit of beverage onto the cement with the urgency of Jorge's brotherly embrace.

"Sorry," she said, sending a sweet, totally insincere smile toward the trio of tomfoolery. "Look at me. Carted off before you can dig into the rest of my personal life."

Rosita waved a chipper bye-bye to them, but Mama and Patrick only seemed to get more thoughtful.

"They had you surrounded," Jorge whispered to her as they entered the house.

While they made their way toward the heady smells of rice, refried beans and chile-spiced vegetables, Christina said, "*Gracias*, Jorge. Something's up their sleeves. Maybe they were getting a feel for my schedule so they can set me up on some disastrous blind dates. Who knows?"

"Hey, I have the feeling I'll be in the same situation as soon as they're done with you. Mama and Rosita can't help themselves from meddling, bless those two bored women."

The sizzle of food, the clanging of pots and the buzz of lively conversation welcomed them to the kitchen. Like the rest of the dwelling, this room was accented with reminders of old Mexico: ranch antiques, such as an old lasso and cowboy hat, hung on the walls; hand-painted tiles decorated the floor; copper implements hung from racks. Steam from the stove added the final touch, lending the area a homey feel.

"Here she is," Jorge said, letting go of Christina. "Safe and sound."

"Oh, good." Sierra, their youngest sister, flashed her compassionate brown eyes at Christina. Her long, curly brown hair was in a ponytail, giving the petite girl a waifish appeal. "We guessed you were being subjected to the third degree."

Gloria, the family beauty queen, with her long, flawless honey-brown hair and perfectly coiffed self, took Christina's wineglass and set it on the counter. As she folded a knife into her sister's hand and set her quickly to work on slicing bell peppers, Gloria's self-designed silver jewelry sang like wind chimes.

"Your effort is appreciated, Jorge," she said.

"Am I being dismissed?" He leaned on the counter, as if playfully rooting himself.

"Yes," said all three sisters.

They knew he didn't enjoy woman-talk anyway, so why not give him an excuse to leave?

"That's ungrateful." He grabbed a fattening hunk of unshredded cheese and bit into it, dashing off to wherever men like him went when there was a family function.

The stables? The TV room? The nearest cliff to hang glide off of?

As he left, Christina swatted at his retreating form

with a nearby towel, missing his hip by inches. On purpose, of course, since she was well-known as the crack-shot toweler of the family.

"So were we right?" Gloria asked, going back to her chore of stirring a simmering pot of beans. "Is Mama up to no good?"

"Just like when she masterminded our reunion by locking us into that room until we all made up?" Sierra added, chopping strawberries.

"Something fishy is going on," said Christina. "But I can't figure out what."

Both sisters nodded, wrinkling their foreheads and turning back to their cooking tasks. While they weren't looking, Christina couldn't help but sneak a piece of that delicious cheddar cheese, too, just like Jorge had done.

So she'd just do a few more sit-ups tonight.

As it happened, she'd barely popped it into her mouth before Sierra glanced back at her.

"Mama's been giving me the marriage eye also, ever since Chad and I split."

"I told you," Gloria said, "stop thinking about that bag of dirt. He only makes you melancholy."

"I know." Sierra's delicate shoulders slumped under the pink cotton of her spring blouse. "But I can't help it. Maybe Chad was my last chance and I'm never going to find a man like him again."

Christina knew exactly how her sis was feeling. Even though she'd had only two notable boyfriends in her life, each breakup had built a monument of sadness for her. An inner mark of memory, keeping her guarded, yet vulnerable.

She'd never been the type to give out hugs, but now, after realizing how much family meant, Christina didn't hesitate to comfort Sierra with an embrace. The younger woman rested her head on Christina's shoulder, driving home that she was a big sister and had so many responsibilities to make up for.

"After our year is over and done with," she said, referring to the bet while petting Sierra's crazy-curled head, "you'll find someone who appreciates everything about you. I'll bet Mr. Right's even closer than you think."

"I wish." Sierra sniffled, then immediately straightened up. "Actually, no. I don't wish. I won't crumble. Not like Gloria did with Jack."

In a show of unity, Christina hugged Sierra closer. *You said it, sister.*

Gloria joined them, stroking her younger sibling's shoulder. "Okay, you two, enough. I had my day of French maid punishment, but Christina's right about one thing. The second you stop looking for love, that's when you'll find it."

Rockwell's charming smile danced over Christina's vision.

Oh, please.

Sierra dried her eyes against Christina's olive T-shirt, but that was okay. A little smudge of tears added some character to her wardrobe anyway, and she could use all she could get.

"Had you stopped looking, Gloria?" Sierra asked. "When you found Jack, I mean?"

"You bet." The loveliest of the Mendoza women became even more so as she laid a hand upon her belly, where a child was growing. "I'd lost all hope. But now, I can't ever believe I felt that way."

"There's a man out there for you, Sierra," Christina added. "Just wait a year and you'll see."

"Same for you." Sierra's innocent eyes shone in the aftermath of her tears. "You're due, Christina."

"No kidding," said Gloria. "Five years is a long time between boyfriends."

There was a pause, and Christina knew just what her sisters were thinking. Macrizon. Rebecca Waters.

When both Gloria and Christina had worked in the same office—Gloria as a CPA, Christina as an analyst—their co-worker had befriended them. Rebecca had been a party girl extraordinaire, taking them clubbing every night, staying out late, encouraging them to show up to work the next morning spent and hungover. Even though Christina had been the eternal designated driver, the friend who'd done more observing than carousing, she'd noticed a fall in her efficiency. And she'd pulled back from Rebecca.

That's when the other woman had taken some mild revenge.

"Don't worry. Nobody like Rebecca will ever come between us again," Gloria said softly.

"I know." Overwhelmed, Christina turned away, resumed slicing the peppers.

But Gloria stopped her by resting a hand on top of Christina's.

"Sis?" she said.

Christina was so used to living her life in a self-imposed shell that it was hard to look up again. But she did.

Gloria was still holding her hand. "You know Rebecca was lying about Carson."

Carson Fuller. A man Christina had started to date after she'd retreated from Rebecca. A good man, who appreciated her brains and told her she was gorgeous and desirable. And even though Christina had a hard time believing the part about her so-called beauty, she'd fallen for Carson.

At the time, Gloria was still partying with Rebecca, caught in a swirling descent of debauchery. There'd been nothing Christina could do to convince her sister to pull away from their co-worker. And when Rebecca had found out that Christina was trying to "steal" Gloria, she'd pitted the sisters against each other.

"Deep down," Christina said, "I knew Rebecca was lying when she kept insinuating that you and Carson were interested in each other. But there was always a small part of me that couldn't help believing it."

"I wish you'd known otherwise."

Same here, thought Christina. Because if she had, they all wouldn't have wasted so much time apart.

"You and I were far beyond having rational conversations at that point," Christina said, remembering how things had gone from bad to worse.

Gloria glanced at her sandals, then back up, regret sheening in her eyes. "I'll never forgive myself for not backing you up with William Dugan."

Christina's stomach turned. It had been the hardest time in her life, with her breaking up with Carson because she'd believed that he was attracted to Gloria. With her reeling under the inappropriate advances of William Dugan.

It'd taken all her strength to press sexual harassment charges against him. And when Rebecca had started spreading rumors that Christina had "asked for it," she'd lost courage. Then she'd had trouble prosecuting Dugan, since his powerful reputation spoke louder than her pitiful, hard-to-prove accusations. The final nail in her coffin had been when Gloria had refused to believe her, too, even hinting that Dugan's harassment was a figment of Christina's imagination.

Soon after the charges against her boss had been dismissed, she'd moved to Los Angeles, mired in shame and distrust.

"I think," said Christina, reaching out for her sister's hands, "we're beyond all that. We're here to move on, right?"

"Right," they said, holding on to each other.

She was so caught up in her sisters that she barely heard the front door open and close.

This is what mattered, she thought, squeezing their fingers in her grip. Family.

Never having anyone come between them again.

But just as she was fighting the happy tears aching in her throat, an interloper stepped in front of her, breaking her hold on Gloria.

"Christina."

Out of breath, Derek Rockwell stood there, brown eyes turned to a deep black, a high flush overcoming the usual tan of his face.

The shock of seeing him electrified Christina, fixing her into one place, speechless. As they locked gazes, her heartbeat thudded in her ears.

But her sisters weren't so overcome.

"Who are you?" Gloria asked.

"That wasn't very polite," Sierra added.

He was frozen, too, and for a second, Christina actually thought he might be just as rattled by seeing her again.

She blinked. He blinked.

Then they both regained their composure.

"I apologize," he said, turning around to face her sisters. "That *was* very rude, but…"

He grabbed Christina's hand and started leading her out of the kitchen.

"Christina?" Gloria asked.

"Just a minute." She tugged away from Rockwell, pointed to him. "This is my boss. Evidently, I'm still on the clock."

Rockwell paused, then flashed that lethal grin at her sisters. Immediately, they both relaxed and smiled right back.

Suckers.

Yeah. As if she were one to talk.

"Derek Rockwell," he said, striding forward to shake their hands. "Again, I apologize."

When the introductions had been completed, he turned back to Christina. Behind him, Sierra and Gloria gave her an enthusiastic thumbs-up. How embarrassing.

"Did you finally decide to join the little people for some fun and games at the barbecue?" she asked.

"Not exactly."

He started to lead her away again, but she dug in her heels. Finally, no doubt realizing she wouldn't be pushed around, Rockwell stopped walking. But he did keep his hand on her elbow.

Fingers against her bare skin. The sensation shot a jumble of awareness through her.

And she couldn't help wondering if he was feeling the same explosions.

Derek didn't want to stop touching her.

This was the most skin he'd ever seen Christina exhibit. Sure, she was wearing a pretty tame T-shirt with shorts and sandals, but he could see actual curves now.

The fluid lines of her hips, her waist, her breasts.

Desire jagged through his belly, and he forced himself to let go of her.

"Why are you here?" she asked.

Because he was a workaholic? Because he'd started

to convince himself that a good presentation would make him shine in Jack's and Patrick's estimations?

He went with the simplest explanation.

"You wouldn't take any of my calls."

"Doesn't that tell you something?"

Whoa. Slightly ticked off.

"I like my employees to always be available," he said. "And I don't like to be ignored."

"Then maybe you should invest in a harem."

In the background, there was the sudden rattling of dishes. Shortly thereafter, Sierra and Gloria whizzed past, carrying plates out of the room.

When they were gone, Derek couldn't help offering a grin to her. Hell, The Rockwell Smile had been getting him out of tough spots with women for years.

"What makes you think I don't already have a harem?" he asked.

"Not only is that wrong in so many ways," she said, planting her hands on her slim hips, "but I'm willing to bet you're being facetious. Now leave."

Hello? The smile? Hadn't she seen it?

He cleared his throat. "You wouldn't come to the office, so I'm here to bring the office to you. I've got the materials in my car."

Her mouth gaped, then she shut it. "You came all the way out here, twenty miles one way from San Antonio, to ruin my day? Did I not say that I would come in tonight?"

"I'm inspired *now*."

"And I'm not. I'm having quality family time, and *no one* disturbs that."

Derek didn't know much about "family time," so he couldn't relate. Except when it came to Patrick, of course, but that was different. They generally didn't have barbecues together.

"I can't do this without you," he said, ignoring her excuses.

Christina closed her eyes, almost looking as if she were going to explode from a lack of patience. Calmly, she said, "You really need to learn the PowerPoint computer program, Rockwell."

Rockwell? At least it was more personal without the "Mr."

Derek couldn't help feeling a certain sense of accomplishment.

"Come on," he said. "I'll run my ideas past you and you can show me the finer points of cyber slide shows."

When she opened her eyes, his heart jumped. God, she was incredibly hot with some anger running through her. Her eyes were a more golden shade, livid with emotion.

"I'm not leaving my family," she said. "Never again. Not even for a day."

Derek didn't want to admit it, but he thought his new idea would be the coup de grâce of their presentation. Impressing his colleagues was all-important, especially since Jack would be in the room.

Spurred by the need to look good at all costs, Derek reacted without thinking.

Earlier, he'd spotted a rope hanging on the wall, a decoration. But he had need of it in an entirely different way now.

He took it down and inspected it.

"What are you doing, Rockwell?"

"You coming?" He looped it, stepped closer to her.

"You wouldn't dare."

As an answer, he slid the lasso over her body. It wasn't tight enough to do damage, but it made moving her arms real tough.

"Very funny," she said, looking as if she were close to blowing her top. "Now take it off."

Instead, he started walking, pulling her along. "I need you, Christina."

"So you said. Look, can't you take no for an answer?"

"I didn't get where I am listening to refusals."

As he guided her through the spacious living room, they ran into Patrick, who'd obviously been summoned by her sisters.

"I'm being kidnapped," Christina said.

"About time," Patrick said, leaning against a wall and smiling.

As Christina's mouth dropped open, Derek shot the older man a chastising glance. "Not another comment, all right?"

"Fair enough." Patrick motioned toward the backyard. "Stay with us and I'll be as quiet as a mouse."

"Nope, too much work to do. That's why you

brought me to San Antonio, right? To get something done?"

While Patrick considered this, Christina interrupted.

"Rockwell, your partner and his wife are requesting your presence. Wouldn't it be a good networking move to stay?"

Hope gleamed in her eyes, but Derek wasn't about to give in. He could let up on their schedules when this was over and done with. If he stayed here, he'd never relax anyway.

Work was the only way to calm him.

From the look on Patrick's face, the older man understood. They'd been partners for too long.

"I wish you'd slow down, Derek," he said softly.

"You know me better than that."

Christina was trying to shrug out of the lasso. In a flash of guilt, Derek almost helped her.

But he wanted her with him. *Needed* her help, damn it.

She caught his gaze and stopped moving. Shaking her head, she seemed to comprehend his urgent hunger to succeed, too.

"*Ay*," she said reluctantly. "I'll come to the darn office. You've got me paranoid that the presentation isn't good enough."

Great, now he was feeling like a real heel. He freed her, more out of shame than anything else.

What had he been thinking?

Patrick was still watching Derek, a slight quirk to his mouth. Why was he looking so smug?

"Just don't work too late kids," he said, traipsing back toward the barbecue.

Both Derek and Christina followed his progress, then stood in silence as the patio door slid closed.

"Well…" she said, walking toward the front door.

"You can stay."

His mouth snapped shut before he could back down any further.

Christina glanced toward where Patrick had disappeared, then at the floor, almost as if she'd realized just how damned much this meant to him.

His heart clenched into itself.

She resumed her progress toward the door, sighing. "Since I'm now as nervous as you are about the presentation, I've got no stomach to stay. I'll meet you at the office. I'd like to have access to the AV equipment instead of working out of your trunk."

"Christina?"

She stopped, hand on the doorknob, but didn't turn around.

"I appreciate…" What? Her understanding?

They didn't know each other enough for that. And they never would.

She opened the door, aiming her next words over her shoulder. "I know. Believe me…I know."

As she left, he didn't say a word.

He'd said too much already.

Chapter Four

At midnight, Derek felt as if there were still a thousand things left to do, even though he and Christina had been working nonstop for hours.

Saturdays usually meant that there were employees in and out of the building all day, but no one else was crazy enough to be in the offices at this time. Thus, the lonely glow of lights and the hum of his and Christina's computers only added to what went unspoken between them.

He glanced up from the spreadsheet he was laboring over, his gaze finding his co-worker yet again, pure lust clutching at his body.

She was sitting on a chair that had been reversed and was slumped over the back of it while reading a community college catalog. Chin resting on a forearm, she moved her lips slightly as she took in the text, as if mouthing the words would make their meaning clearer. A sure sign of her tiredness.

Her hair was still up, of course, but tonight she'd used a leather thong with a wooden stick to fashion a bun with strands spiking out of it. A looser style, he thought.

And she'd kicked off her sandals long ago, the casual gesture making Derek wonder how she'd look walking around his bedroom, barefoot and clad in one of his own shirts, hair tumbled.

Caught up in the image, Derek sat back in his chair, running a hand over his smile.

"Pecos Community College has a good program," she said, still inspecting the catalog.

"It's close by, too," he said.

This was part of his big idea: offering college-level financial classes to the employees for credit, which would go toward salary raises.

Earlier, after he and Christina had arrived at Fortune-Rockwell in their separate cars, he'd tried to make her forget about his hotheaded me-man-you-employee act by explaining the positives of his new plan. Luckily, she'd bought into it right away, immediately getting to work and seeming to forget that he'd literally roped her in here.

He just wasn't used to reacting so strongly to the word *no*. Probably because he wasn't used to hearing it.

"So what do you think?" he asked. "Would the college dean be open to chatting with us at this time of night? It'd be worth his while to hear us out."

Christina shot him a half-amused, lowered gaze over the top of the catalog. "Not everyone is at your beck and call. You need to learn some boundaries, Rockwell, even if I was stupid enough to give in to you just this once."

"Maybe I can get a hold of him tomorrow to talk specifics, then we can run from there. Think we need to call in Twyla, Jonathan and Seth to help us out?"

"Our team needs to enjoy their weekend." Putting down the catalog, Christina shut her eyes, then raised her hands over her head, arching her back. "We can handle this ourselves, if you can refrain from acting entitled."

Ya-ow.

As she stretched, her small, firm breasts pressed against her olive T-shirt. He could almost feel them in his hands, the tips aroused and beaded against his palms.

He could imagine slipping his hand into the curved small of her back, gently bending her away, shaping her so she'd fit against his own body, skin-to-skin under the moonlight.

Damn. The agony of wanting her when she was only a few feet away, the knowledge that he wasn't going to have her.

Not if he was a smart businessman.

"Okay," she said, ending the stretch and rubbing

her eyes. "We've adjusted the slide presentation to our best ability tonight. And it looks like we need to get hold of Pecos College's administration before we go any further. Should we line up some alternative colleges, just in case Pecos refuses?"

Time to get his mind back on work, eh? "We probably should."

But both of them just sat there, exhausted.

"We could take a break," he said.

"Too much to do."

"Right."

Still, neither of them moved.

Instead, he fixed his gaze on her laptop, which was stranded on the cushions of his leather couch. The screen saver—a picture of a gigantic ice cream sundae swirled with rainbow colors—hypnotized him.

Better to look there than at Christina, he thought.

But then he started thinking about the comparisons. Christina. Ice cream.

Both of them would taste real sweet.

"Well, I'll be licked," she said.

Flinching, Derek turned his attention toward her.

She was inspecting her cell phone, which she'd explained earlier was always set on silent mode during marathon work sessions.

"Sierra called three times." Christina laughed. "I'm sure she wants to know if I'm safe from your overzealous charm."

"What, she doesn't trust me?"

"Rockwell, you lassoed me."

He smoothed a hand over his hair. "I can't say I've ever tried that method of getting someone to work. But it was highly effective."

"You're just fortunate I have a sense of humor."

There was something about the tone of her voice that gave him pause.

"I know. You're right, Christina. You have my deepest apologies."

She hesitated. "I appreciate that, Rockwell."

Last name again. Somehow, he'd been hoping that the hushed office and the midnight hour would lend themselves to some humanization.

Giving up, he said, "Maybe you ought to call Sierra's voice mail, tell her that your big bad boss is treating you with kid gloves."

"Are you referring to this torture by sleep deprivation?" Christina shut her phone, stuffed it back into her bag. "That's kid-glove treatment?"

Derek held back from elaborating on just how he wanted to be treating her:

Warm candlelight.

Soft sheets.

Hot kisses.

"Besides," she continued, amazingly oblivious to the rise in his body temperature, "I called home on my way here. Gloria answered, and I told her not to worry."

"Worry?" he asked, trying to appear innocent. "With me? A family couldn't want more for their little girl."

Christina raised her eyebrows. "You think a lot of yourself, don't you?"

Derek shrugged. "I'm not such an awful guy."

"Oh, you're not a corporate wolf, huh? Patrick seems inordinately proud of your feral instincts. Your tear-'em-up reputation."

She had to be talking about his business calling card, because Derek wouldn't have said the same thing when it came to females. Sure, he wasn't exactly a one-woman guy, but he liked to think he treated the fairer persuasion with appreciation—even if the relationships didn't last long.

"Patrick helped me become a success," he said. "I'm sort of a younger version of him, I guess."

Except for the part where Patrick was head over heels for one woman—his wife, Lacey.

Christina's gaze softened, and Derek's chest got tight, numb with wanting to actually deserve such an admiring look from her.

"You and Patrick have a bond," she said. "I can tell. Is that why…"

"What?" Did she want to ask about his tension with Jack?

"Nothing."

She stood from her chair, glancing away from him.

"Is Patrick the reason Jack and I have that sibling rivalry going?" he finished for her.

"I'm tired, and my mouth is running before my brain can catch up. You don't have to answer if you don't want to."

As she moved toward his desk, all lean grace, with those long, bare legs and sun-toasted skin, she touched the picture of his mom and her dogs. It took all his strength not to put it facedown on his desk, turn his past away from this woman as he'd done the other day.

Besides, something about the dead of night encouraged him to tell her about himself. But why? Derek never talked about his family to anyone—except Patrick.

So he was incredulous when the words spilled out.

"Patrick really helped me," he said. "I was purposely aimless as a kid."

Still, he wouldn't tell her everything, like how his rebellion had been in reaction to all of Sir's rules and regulations.

He continued. "Even so, just as soon as I could, I joined the Marines, right out of high school."

Christina leaned against the side of his desk, crossed one leg over the other. She was close enough so he could catch the shine of deep red polish on her toenails.

Red. So that's the color she'd been hiding under her usual business-day pumps.

"I guessed it," she said. "Even on that first day, I thought there was something precise about you. Your hair, your clothes. Very regimented."

A spark of anger lit through Derek. Is that how she saw him? A reflection of Sir?

"You've got a naturally commanding presence," she added.

Then she looked down, and Derek knew she'd given away too much of her opinions to him.

Quelling the rage of his memories, he tentatively reached out to tug on her T-shirt. She startled, but didn't move away.

"I don't seem to scare you *too* much," he said.

She didn't respond to his comment. Instead, she turned back to him, redirected the subject.

"And how did you get from the Marines to Fortune-Rockwell?"

He drew his fingers back from her shirt, keeping his hand in front of him on the desk. "I had a short stint in the military. Basically…"

He thought of how he would glance at himself in the mirror and see a man in uniform. A man who looked too much like his father.

After the mirror epiphany, he'd quit the Corps as soon as possible.

Derek's fingers tightened around a pen. "Basically, in school, I'd liked math, and I was always the guy who had some kind of scheme to get rich. So it made sense for me to learn more about business. That's how I ended up with an MBA at Columbia."

"Not bad," she said.

Her respect made him kind of giddy. Or maybe he was just too tired to think straight.

"Then I met Patrick at a mentor dinner. Our philosophies meshed and, soon afterward, I went to work for him at Fortune Banking. It wasn't long until the business evolved into Fortune-Rockwell."

And, from there, he'd become the toast of New York. Charity functions, galas, the opera… He attended them all, with the gossip columns capturing a new beauty on his arm every time he hit the town.

Where had that guy gone?

"You're lucky," she said, "to have found a friend in Patrick. My family feels the same way."

"He's one in a million."

The conversation dwindled, and he searched for something to say. He was afraid she'd hop up from his desk to blurt, "All rightie, then. Enough talk. Time to get back to college catalogs."

But she surprised him by laughing instead.

A low, sultry sound—something you might hear as a bow moved over the strings of a cello.

She was staring at his loosened collar with those forever-deep hazel eyes. Irises that hid libraries of knowledge, years of wisdom that she'd experienced in her short life.

"Um, your…" She gestured with her hand.

He looked down, pulled at his collar and discovered that wrinkle again. Each morning it started out straight, perfect. But somehow, during the day, the material curled, thwarting his best efforts.

When he glanced back up at her, he snared her gaze with his. The throb of an endless heartbeat pulsed between them.

She reached over.

With slow care, she folded the linen back where it belonged.

"It was distracting me," she said, her voice throaty. Different from the normally clipped, professional tone of Christina Mendoza, business analyst.

Now, she was just a woman.

And he was a man.

Alone together on a Saturday night.

He didn't even breathe for fear of reminding her that her fingertips were still brushing his collar. The heat of her skin lingering so close to his neck turned him inside out, exposing a side of himself he always kept locked away.

Did she see the unguarded desire in his eyes? The terrifying curiosity of wanting to know what it was like to be with a woman who had great substance?

Maybe she did because, before his heart could beat again, she'd pulled away, stood, walked toward her computer on the couch.

Dammit, why hadn't he made a move on her?

From the way she'd been acting, he could've had her. Could've been stripping off her T-shirt, her shorts.

Could've been kissing his way down her body.

What was so different about this woman that he hadn't taken advantage of the fleeting intimacy?

She'd thrown him off guard for some reason. He just wasn't used to easy touches, drawn-out beats of uncertain tension.

Tender gestures.

As she sat down on the couch, attention suddenly glued to her computer, Derek longed to make a joke of what had just happened. To ease the obvious discomfort.

But if there was one thing he knew about this woman already, it was that she was incredibly skittish about compliments and intimate office situations.

He'd forget about what had happened.

It was the best solution.

Determined to erase his emotions, he tapped at the keyboard, but it did no good.

The new awareness filtering the room wouldn't lift.

It was only when his cell phone rang that he felt halfway relieved.

Yet, when he checked to see who was calling at this hour, he cursed. She was the last person he needed to talk with right now.

And a perfect way to get his mind off Christina, he supposed.

Remember the bet. Remember Gloria in a French maid suit...

Oh, did Christina ever have to convince herself to stay here, rooted to the couch. She'd do anything to keep from dashing back over to Rockwell and wrestling him to the floor in a love hug.

When his phone rang, it was as if her senses had slammed right back into her from wherever the heck they'd been vacationing.

Now, she was just trying to get back to normal.

Peace. Calm. Yoga breathing.

Good. Now that she had it together, she could berate herself for how dumb she'd been.

Touching his collar?

Granted, it hadn't been as if she'd licked him up and down like a lollipop, but the gesture had been just as obvious.

Never again, she thought.

Just remember William Dugan.

As a matter of fact, maybe it'd even be a good idea for Christina to go home. Time had gotten away from her, and she hadn't given a second thought to how an isolated nighttime work session with her boss would look.

All right. She'd wait for him to get off the phone and check out for the night. Then she could take some work home until tomorrow, when daylight would bring other employees into the office, just like she'd seen today.

Although she was being cautious, Christina would get through this without having to deal with rumors or more Rebecca Waters–type insinuations that could damage a business reputation.

From Rockwell's position behind the desk, he cursed, giving Christina an excuse to look at him.

He was staring at his ringing phone, frowning. She wanted to ask who it was and why the call put him on edge, but she refrained, thinking she'd already been way too forward tonight.

Punchy. *Si*, that was why she'd lost control. Lack

of sleep had frazzled her nerves as well as her common sense.

Relieved to have justified her behavior, she accessed an Internet search engine so she could absorb herself in local community colleges. But her attention wavered.

Especially when Rockwell answered his phone.

"Derek, here."

There was a pause as the person on the other line talked. While Christina pretended not to peek at his reaction, he kept his demeanor unconcerned, unemotional.

Dios Mio, what a babe. Even as worn out as he was from their night of labor, he still came off as arrogant and self-possessed as ever.

As he answered the caller, she saw a shift in his expression. A firmness. A darkening of his brown eyes to black.

Was it her imagination, or did his irises actually change color when he was agitated or angry?

Ooo, that was intriguing.

"Chantelle, we talked about this," he said.

Christina whipped her attention back to the computer.

Chantelle. Wasn't that some kind of $100-an-ounce perfume that smelled like seventy-year-old socialites lunching in the Foo-Foo Room?

Rockwell got out of his seat and made his way toward the personal suite attached to his office.

"I know you do. But I'm working in San Antonio now." Pause. "I don't know when I'm coming back."

Ah-ha. Okay. If Christina hadn't caught onto it before, she had now. Chantelle was a girlfriend from New York. Or maybe not a girlfriend anymore.

At any rate, she felt strongly enough about Rockwell to be calling him in the middle of the night.

As he shut the door, she heard him say, "No, I'm not with anybody right now."

Her heart sank. She was that "nobody" he was with.

Hadn't he seen her offer him a tiny piece of her heart earlier?

Figures. That's where touching men's collars got you. Ignore-o-ville.

She couldn't hear the rest of Chantelle's long-distance booty call because the suite was well insulated from the outer office. So Christina settled into a more comfortable position on the couch, lying on her side.

Might as well get some work done while Rockwell was messing around with personal issues.

But the screen only blurred in front of her eyes, even as she tried valiantly to keep them open.

Before she could stop the inevitable, she drifted off to a well-earned sleep, dreaming of stolen touches, passionate kisses, hungry moans of faraway pleasure.

Dreaming of Derek.

The attached suite included a changing room filled with Derek's extra business wardrobe and gym gear, a shower with all the required supplies and a restroom.

This was where Derek was at the moment, propped against the marble sink counter, one arm crossed over his chest as if to ward off Chantelle from across the miles.

"I miss you so much," she said in a husky, one-pack-a-day voice.

He'd gone out with her once before being transferred from New York. Actually, his relocation had offered a good excuse to say a graceful goodbye to this particular Lite, because even after just one encounter, she'd grown way too possessive. Still, she'd been calling him off and on for a month now, and as lonely as he'd been for female company, he'd flirted with her over the airwaves.

But now, he knew it was time to end it.

"I won't be back for a while," he said, trying to let her down gently.

He didn't want to say what was really on his mind: *I'm just not interested. At all.*

"Maybe," she said teasingly, "we can pass the time by, you know, getting close right now."

Phone sex? Christina was in the next room. Chantelle's idea was definitely out of the question.

"In all honesty, Chantelle, I'm working. There's a presentation I've got to get done by Monday."

"What are you wearing?" she asked, undaunted.

He could almost see the redhead lounging on her bed, a half glass full of champagne losing its bubbles on the nightstand next to her, her curvy body covered by nothing more than a pink teddy.

From her reputation, he hadn't expected her to become clingy, but that was the danger of acting like a playboy, he guessed. Sometimes the women changed their minds about the rules after they'd accepted them.

"Thanks, Chantelle," he said. "But…"

For his own peace of mind, he had to put an end to all these midnight calls. "…I'm seeing someone."

Silence on the other end of the line.

Derek began to pace. "We talked about our night together being just that—one night."

"Who is she?"

Here it went. "You don't know her. She's a business associate and…"

"Go on."

Derek smiled, thinking of the woman sitting on his couch. "I'm crazy about her."

"For the time being, right?"

Chantelle was challenging him, probably wondering why he all of a sudden had decided to change his MO and stick with one woman.

"Right," he said, reminding himself that he never took relationships seriously. "For the time being."

"It doesn't sound like a big deal. I could fly out there and—"

"Chantelle." He sighed. "There's nothing between us. You're a beautiful woman who's got a lot to give a man who can settle down. But you know I'm not that guy."

"I was just hoping…"

"I'm sorry."

With a sound of fury, she hung up on him.

As he made his way back to the office, Derek shut off his own phone, drained. Disgusted with himself for the first time since he'd started dating.

What had happened to the fun? The old times, when he could be with a woman and they'd romance the night away, only to leave in the morning with a sweet goodbye and a clear understanding that it was over before it'd begun?

He stepped into the office proper, ready to bury himself in work again.

But that's when he saw her.

Christina, cuddled on his couch, hands tucked under her head as she slept. One of her legs was curled over the other, causing her cute rump to stick out.

In that instant, Derek's heart cracked.

Quietly, he bent near her, getting his fill of her serenity. There was no urgency to her right now, no sense of prim expectancy.

No, at the moment her lips were pursed in soft slumber, her dark lashes winging against rosy cheeks.

Unable to stop himself, Derek ran a forefinger over the hollow of her cheekbone, a foreign tingle running up his arm and to his chest.

He wanted to stay here all night, just watching her, just feeling this contented buzz. But what would he do if she woke up to find him hovering?

The consequences wouldn't be helpful to their working relationship, that was for sure.

Smacked back to reality, he stood, then went to the wardrobe closet to get the pillow and blanket that he used when he pulled office overnighters.

With the utmost care, he slipped the down cushion under her head, freezing when she moaned and stirred. As she shifted position, her mouth came to rest against his bared arm, and the contact sent a jolt through him.

Pulse hammering, he concentrated on covering her with the blanket, one-handed. Then, not quite wanting to move yet, he sat there, feeling her breath caress his skin.

Minutes passed—enough time for the inevitable guilt to rattle him. To convince him to remove his arm, inch by agonizing inch, from beneath her head.

Then, telling himself to act like a real boss, he retreated to his chair and closed his eyes.

Fully guarded once again.

Chapter Five

Christina was awakened by the aroma of fresh coffee and the sting of sunlight pouring through office windows.

Office windows?

Disoriented, she caught her breath and sat up to survey her surroundings.

A few potted plants. World-beat instruments. Massive desk. Big, empty boss chair.

With Sierra sitting in it.

What? Christina closed her eyes, then opened them again.

"Buenos dias," her youngest sister said, dressed in a white, flower-sprigged sundress, her curly hair pulled back.

Bright and fresh.

"The last time I looked," Christina said, "you were a social worker, not a corporate shark named Rockwell. Where is he?"

"Gone when I got here. I didn't want to wake you up, so I waited, but not for long." Sierra got out of her seat and put down the college catalog she'd been using to pass the time. "Sis, you never returned my calls last night."

"I wanted to, but I crashed." A little more awake now, Christina could actually formulate some questions. "Not that I'm unhappy to see you, but why are you in this office?"

"Gloria said you were alone with Derek, and no one answered at your condo, so I thought I'd just check on you here. And...ta-da!"

She motioned toward a table by the doorway. It held a bag, a carton with cups and a grease-stained box.

Christina's mouth started to water, and she realized that her stomach was hollow. Her food cravings almost overcame her misgivings about Sierra coming to check up on her.

It was just like her *hermanita* to concern herself with everyone else's problems. Having Sierra show up at the crack of dawn wasn't all that much of a surprise.

Years ago, when Christina and Gloria had been fighting, Sierra had performed this same nurturing wake-up routine with each of them. Not only had their little sister been worried about both of them, but she suffered from insomnia.

Poor, fretful Sierra.

As Christina headed toward the food, just to inspect what was there, of course, she said, "How did you manage to get past security downstairs?"

"Patrick arranged clearance."

"Helpful, that Patrick." She lifted the plastic lid off one of the cups, and the rich steam of gourmet coffee floated out. But Christina didn't drink the stuff. Not in public at least. It was terrible for the body.

"There's green tea for you," Sierra said. "But I thought Derek might like some fresh brew."

Her sister came to the table and started to unload the treats: frosted doughnuts, éclairs, breakfast burritos.

If Christina wasn't careful, she'd drool all over her shirt. But she could avoid temptation. All kinds, if necessary.

Finding a bran muffin, she peeled away the paper lining. Mmm, so nutritious.

She could always eat a doughnut later, alone, when no one else was around. Junk food tasted much better in secret, anyway.

Christina cleared her materials from the couch and set them on the floor, making room for Sierra. Her sister had a plate full of baked goods.

"There's a lot left for Derek," she said, and from the way she was pursing her lips, Christina knew that she had a load of questions waiting to be asked.

"I accidentally fell asleep, Sierra," she said, steeping the tea bag in her hot water. "Nothing happened. You know how I feel about office shenanigans."

Or how she used to feel, at least.

"Even after the way he whisked you away from us yesterday?"

"Granted, his method of getting me here was extreme, but it was all business."

Most of it, anyway. Except for that moment when she'd been the one to overstep the lines she'd drawn.

But there was still room to go back. He hadn't responded to her collar groping, so maybe it wasn't even something she should be worrying about.

"It's just…" Sierra hesitated. "I was surprised you stayed the night here. Especially after what happened with your sexual harassment charges against William Dugan."

"This isn't one of my shiniest moments, I'll tell you that. Neither of us was paying attention to the time, and I was going to leave. Really I was."

"Don't be so hard on yourself. You're wary, and you have every right to be."

Christina knew that, but she didn't want to be neurotic about her office relationships. And she didn't want to go overboard, documenting every interaction or being so closed-off that she was impossible to work with. Ultimately, she reasoned, treating every man as if he were a potential harasser only made the true cases weaker.

But she still had to consider her business reputation.

"I made a bad call last night," she said. "It definitely won't happen again."

She ate some of the muffin, putting an end to a conversation she'd rather forget.

"I believe you." Sierra took a sip of coffee, made a face, then added sweetener. "Unlike Gloria, I just don't want you to become the next victim of our bet."

Chewing, Christina merely sent a quizzical glance to her sister.

Sierra nodded. "Uh-huh. She thinks there's something going on between you and the boss, and she's already planning your punishment for losing."

"Knowing Gloria, it'll be devious."

"It'll be something public. Something dirty, since she's still sore about having to clean our houses."

Gloria had always encouraged Christina to shed her shyness, and there was no doubt her scheme would include this angle, too.

"Then I'll have to make sure I don't fall to man temptation," Christina said, drinking some tea.

Though she sounded casual, she was really thinking that, for something that should've been so easy to do, winning the bet sounded awfully tough.

A whole year of not dating men.

Before now, it'd never been a big deal.

"Then, there it is." Sierra stuck out her hand. "The two of us won't give in, even if Gloria couldn't help herself. Shake on it."

Christina did, and the two sisters laughed, knowing how ridiculous everyone no doubt thought it was to be betting on this type of thing.

But, to them, it was all-important. Giving up men would enhance their lives.

They ate and moved on, chatting about the barbecue, about the happiness of becoming aunts to Gloria's child, about Sierra's circle of friends and her frustrations with one of them in particular—Alex Calloway, who always seemed to give her grief.

Christina got the feeling there was more to Sierra's talk than she would admit to, but she let it go for the time being.

However, she'd keep an eye on her sister, just as well as Sierra was monitoring her.

While they were enjoying each other's company, a few drop-in employees wandered into the office, equipped with that sense every nine-to-fiver cultivated for finding treats, no matter where they were hidden.

It was nice to see that she and Rockwell might not be entirely alone, since there were other weekend warriors here, as well.

But just as she was getting more comfortable, Rockwell himself stepped through the doorway—a Rockwell who was a whole lot different from the one she was used to seeing.

He wore athletic shoes; loose, gray sweatpants and a blue tank top that sweat had molded to his muscular chest. Perspiration coated his tanned, strong arms, his face, his hair.

Christina's determination to avoid man temptation screeched to a burning halt.

"Morning," he said, flashing that sidelong grin at them. "I was hoping to sneak past Christina while she was still sleeping."

Then he turned "The Grin" on her, subjecting her to the full force of his charm. She gulped down the last of the bran muffin she'd been demolishing.

Caramba.

Wow, wow, wow.

What was it about him that made Christina want to drop her defenses and paste herself all over his bod?

Hold off, girl, just hold off of him.

While Sierra greeted Rockwell, Christina realized that one side of her hair bun had dipped down and what little makeup she used was probably off her face by now. She tried to fade into the couch cushions, just to see if she could get away with him not picking up on those humbling details.

Sierra was talking. "We've got a bunch of food for you. I'm sure you're hungry after working out. Were you jogging? Christina loves to jog, too."

"Nah, we've got a rowing machine in our company gym, if you could call it that. Christina, we might want to think of expanding it for employee morale and healthier workers. What do you think?"

She managed to move her head up and down, still trying to hide.

"Rowing?" Sierra sat up in her seat. "If you like putting paddles in the water, San Antonio's the place for you. Did you know we've got the Texas Water Safari every May? You can enter the canoeing competition."

"I already have." Rockwell started walking toward his personal suite. "First thing I did when Patrick asked me to move here. I used to be on the heavyweight crew team back at Columbia, and I row every morning, even if it's on a machine. I'm addicted."

"Just like Christina." Sierra swatted her sister on the leg. "Another exercise hound."

Averting her face, she got up from the couch. No lipstick, no eye makeup. Not good.

"Speaking of which," Christina said, walking toward the other side of the room where she'd put her belongings, "I'm due for a workout back home."

"Sounds like a plan," said Rockwell. "I'm taking a shower, digging into Sierra's banquet, then getting to the project again. You coming back here today?"

Actually, she was still on the whole "I'm taking a shower" part.

Rockwell. No clothes. Water beading on his skin, sluicing over muscles, making him even more slick and dangerous.

Her conscience batted at her. Should she work in this semideserted office with him again? Especially with these horn-dog thoughts running through her head?

"We're just about done," he added.

"Maybe we could have a change of scenery," she said, slipping into her sandals and thinking about the other employees whose presence could keep her libido on the straight and narrow. "Maybe we could work in my office this afternoon."

Unlike his buried alcove, her place was in the midst of the floor plan, the windows giving her a view of a lobby with other private offices surrounding it.

"Sure," he said, sounding happy to accommodate her.

Suddenly, she felt like a fool for being so cautious. "Then expect me at about eleven."

That'd leave her enough time for some jogging, yoga, a shower, then Mass.

"I'd like to get home as early as possible," she added, "to gear up for tomorrow's big day."

"Sounds perfect."

Without glancing at him—Lord help her—Christina jetted out of the office, Sierra trailing behind her after bidding Rockwell goodbye.

"What's your rush?" her sister asked as they settled into the elevator.

"I want to get started. Too much to do."

It sounded reasonable.

Besides, telling Sierra that Christina needed a cold shower right away would've been far too telling.

Because she was going to win this bet.

And keep her self-respect.

The afternoon melted into a glorious twilight, and as it spilled through Christina's office window, the room was bathed in orange and red.

The colors mingled over her hair, Derek noted, as he watched her from the love seat. The shades turned her upswept tresses into shimmers of dark, exotic rain.

When he was a kid, he'd seen something similar while his father had been stationed in South Korea.

One night, after Sir had gotten on Derek's ass because he'd found a speck of spaghetti sauce on the dishes his son had washed, Derek had run into the rain, finding the darkest possible corner of the base. He'd watched it fall, how it sparkled and disappeared just as soon as it hit the ground.

Too bad Sir couldn't cease to exist in just the same way, Derek had thought.

But, being too young to strike out on his own, he'd gone home. He always did—until it was legally possible for him to join the Marines.

Yeah, smart choice, wasn't it? He'd chosen the Corps because Sir was in the Army, and Derek had known how much it'd tick off the old man. Sir had despised the Marines, calling them "Bullet Meat" and "Jarheads."

It'd given Derek great pleasure to cause his dad that much consternation.

Until Derek realized how much like Sir he'd become.

At that point, he'd worked hard to establish his own identity, going into business with Patrick, proving that he didn't need Sir's rigid structures by dating woman after woman.

Derek blocked out the thought of the man by diving into his work once again, erasing the past with a parade of numbers and details.

And, soon, he and Christina were ready to do a final run-through of tomorrow's adjusted presentation.

They set up in a conference room and, when they were ready, Christina took a spot near the slide screen while Derek pretended to be an observer. He'd have a minimal amount to say tomorrow, preferring instead to allow his employee to take the reins and quote statistics while both of them fielded questions.

She started PowerPoint, and he sat back to enjoy the show, ready to take notes about any adjustments they'd need to make.

For a woman who'd initially come off as cold and shy, she had commanding stage presence. Even if she was wearing khaki shorts and a blue blouse, Christina Mendoza was an erudite professional.

But there was something more, too. A red-carpet grace, a sense of white-gloved class that most women didn't possess.

Derek couldn't keep his eyes off of her.

The presentation went off without a hitch and, judging from the glow on her face, she damned well knew it.

"Well?" she asked.

"I took some notes. You'll want to read them."

She did a double take. "What did I do that wasn't perfect?"

There was that career cockiness, which didn't seem to suit her reserved personality.

Tossing the notepad on the table, he pointed to it. "Just read."

She rushed right over, clearly ready to tell him why their presentation didn't need retooling again. But she loosened up when she spied what he'd written: You were *amazing*.

A smile lit over her mouth, brightening her face until Derek warmed up just from the look of it. Then she poised her hands over her head.

"Yes!"

Derek laughed, liking this freed spirit. Every day brought more surprises from this woman, made her less removed and untouchable.

"Yes, yes, yes!" She wiggled her hips a little, doing an impromptu dance.

"What's that?" he asked.

"Salsa. Hot mama, lovely, I'm-done-with-this-presentation salsa!"

Well, he could certainly get used to watching this, her bottom waving back and forth in a smooth groove as she kept time to the musical celebration in her mind.

"Don't you love it?" she asked.

"Oh, yeah."

She stopped her dancing, face flushed. "Not that, Rockwell. I'm talking about the rush you get when you realize you're going to kick some caboose for dollars."

Forget corporate profit. All Derek wanted was to see the look on Jack Fortune's face.

Dammit, why'd he have to feel like a kid with a one-size-too-big batting helmet slumped over his sight, staring at the bleachers and waving to his big brother?

Because it'd be great to hit that home run and watch while Jack acknowledged how good he was.

Christina was still flittering around, high on success. "They say analysts are bad for employee morale in general. Humph. Take *that* whoever 'they' are. Pow!" She pretended to slap an invisible face.

Getting out of his seat, he said, "You're practically drunk with joy."

"I get like this." She was slightly panting, holding a hand to her heart. "When I got home and went jogging this morning, I felt it. I know you feel it, too, after you row. The endorphins, kicking right in. I can't get enough of them."

As he moved closer to her, his heart started pulsing, much like it did during his exercise sessions. But this was different, if not just as addictive.

This was fear and desire wrapped around each other.

This was an unquenchable thirst in the face of a tall, cool drink waiting and within his reach.

Christina reached up and touched her hair. For a second, Derek thought she was about to set it free, to allow it to tumble to her shoulders.

His breath hitched in anticipation.

But she merely patted a loose strand back into the shimmery blue clip that was holding it captive.

"Sorry for acting like such a crazy fool," she said, a glint in her eye, "but I need to let off steam. Getting just a few hours of sleep will do that to a person. This is like an all-nighter in college, when you're working like a demon to get a project completed for the next day's due date. Or when you've finished finals…"

Or, he asked himself, when you were so damned sexually frustrated that jumping around was the only way to release the pressure?

Sure, he knew how that felt.

"If it weren't such a bad idea," she added, getting squirrelly again, "I'd give you a dancing lesson."

"You're right. Dancing and getting loose at the office is completely inappropriate."

Christina shot him a knowing glance. "That's not what I mean."

So they were back to employee and boss.

And here he thought they'd made some personal progress, even though Derek knew he shouldn't want it—for more reasons than just keeping his hands off his subordinate.

He recalled how sad his mom had been, waiting for her Army husband to return from the far corners of the earth.

Commitment stunk, all right. And Christina Mendoza wasn't the type of woman who came without that sort of price attached.

Even Derek wasn't a good enough negotiator to avoid that caveat.

"Before you get too happy," he said, turning to the next page of his notes, "maybe you should read this."

Breath coming in deep gasps, Christina stilled her private party, then crept toward the table again, peeking at the paper.

He'd written a couple of things that required finetuning: the pacing of the slides, a typo that reflected an inaccurate pricing quote from when they'd gotten hold of the Pecos College dean today.

"And the next page," he added.

When she looked at it, her smile returned. She no doubt realized that the troubleshooting would be insignificant.

On the last piece of paper, he'd written: You're going to blow them away.

"You scared me to death!" she said, jumping up and grabbing his button-down shirt while pulling him toward her in a show of excited frustration.

Flying high, Christina was hardly even aware of what she was doing. All she knew was that she was happy. Reckless with the exhilaration of success.

She could do anything! And she had, putting together a damned good presentation in record time.

As Derek's dark eyes widened, she even felt a bit more power at his surprise. The scent of him—a tinge of clear, crisp new money and heady musk—spiked her good-girl hormones, throwing them off-kilter.

Before she could tell herself to stop, she was impetuously pulling him down to her, crushing her mouth to his.

For a second, he stiffened, but something buried, something deeply tamed within Christina took this as a challenge.

She could control a man for once. Bring him to his knees instead of the other way around. Couldn't she?

Christina increased the urgency of the kiss, wanting so badly to know that he would give in.

Then, just as she was losing confidence, patience, Derek reacted, echoing the insistent pressure of her lips. He placed a hand at the base of her head to urge her closer, slid his other hand to the small of her back, where his fingers clenched her blouse as if his life depended on it.

Ecstatic, she moaned against him, encouraging his willingness by fisting his hair, seeking, devouring.

As her breasts pressed against his chest, her own body echoed the rise and fall of his breathing, the extent of a shared mindless hunger.

And his head *was* bursting with confusion, a passion he couldn't contain.

The ice queen was kissing him.

How had this happened?

No time to analyze. Who cared anyway? She was excited, and he sure as hell wasn't going to push her away.

But how could he explain the need to take her in his arms, to hold her against him so she wouldn't back away? Because he knew she would, and the knowledge of it ached, made him burn and long to possess her.

Yet Derek didn't work that way. He didn't keep something once he had it. That's why he'd jumped at the chance to move from New York to San Antonio. There'd been too many roots forming, attaching him to a lifestyle that was becoming a habit.

And the act of wrapping his arms around her was too reminiscent of something like ivy, clinging.

Needing something outside of itself to stay standing.

To survive.

Belly fisting, Derek took one last moment to enjoy the scent of her clean hair. The smoothness of her skin. The heat of her lips.

With something close to regret, he ended the kiss, their mouths remaining a whisper apart.

"That was a real moment of insanity," he said, trying to play off the situation.

His heartbeat was loud enough to shake the room.

Obviously mortified, Christina's skin blazed a bright red as she turned and walked away from him. She crossed her arms over her chest, looking for all the world as if she were shivering in the cold in front of a house that she'd been locked out of.

"Whoo." She tried to laugh. "You're right. Not enough sleep."

Relieved by her willingness to take this less than seriously, Derek agreed. "Too much coffee."

"Or tea."

They both nodded thoughtfully, unwilling to move and force the truth out of its hiding place.

"Well." He shoved his hands into his pants pockets. "We should rest up for tomorrow. Big day. You good to go?"

"Definitely."

While she slowly walked to the door, he stayed in the room, wanting to allow her to leave the building first. To give her room.

But then she turned around, mouth opened to say something.

Frozen, Derek hoped she wasn't about to remind him of what had just happened. He was too afraid of what he might say back to her.

She must have read his fear, his doubts. "'Night, Rockwell."

"'Night."

She paused, sighed, then left him standing there, playing that kiss over and over in his mind like a flag that wouldn't stop snapping in the wind.

Finally, the place went dark.

Clearly, the sensor had detected that there wasn't any life left in the room.

Chapter Six

"Damn him."

It was Monday, just moments after the presentation and, already, Derek was on fire. As he burst into the small lobby of his office, his assistant glanced up from her desk.

"Mr. Rockwell? What's wrong?"

Regretting that he couldn't restrain his disappointment, Derek made an effort to calm himself.

"Nothing I can't get over, Dora. Any messages?"

She bestowed a sympathetic smile on him and handed over some papers. "No urgent calls or summons. How did the presentation go?"

Derek bristled, but hoped he didn't show it. "Really well. Our audience loved what we had to say and, in fact, they want more ideas."

So why was he cranky?

After accepting Dora's "Good job, Mr. Rockwell," and walking into his office, he admitted that he knew the reason.

Jack, naturally.

During the postpresentation briefing session, Derek's new partner had basically congratulated Christina on being the driving force behind the concept of personal development. He'd even heaped praise on the rest of the team.

Yet he'd all but ignored Derek's contributions.

Not that Christina and the team didn't deserve acknowledgment. Derek wasn't begrudging anyone—especially their business analyst—that. And she'd taken great pains to give credit to Derek. But, dammit, just once he'd like Jack to say, "You did a hell of a job, Derek."

But maybe he was being ridiculous. So what if his ego had been wounded? He wasn't thirteen anymore, under the thumb of Sir, always seeking impossible approval.

He'd move on and get over it.

So he did, in the best way he knew how—by settling into work, developing ideas for the next phase of the personal development project: constructing "game rooms" and "creative rooms" in order to promote employee productivity.

But just as he was warming up his computer, in strolled Christina.

The gorgeous woman he'd been trying to think of as "his employee" since last night.

Dressed in a deep purple suit, she was riding the wave of success, still glowing, containing whatever overwhelming urges that had caused her to kiss him.

God, if only they were in a different place, in a different situation.

He wouldn't mind another of those lip-locks.

Without thinking, he leaned back in his chair, running a hand over his mouth to erase a grin of provocative reminiscence.

"You scooted off before we could catch you," she said, hands behind her back, body swaying back and forth playfully as if she had something to hide.

"Why linger? Jack didn't have much to say to me."

Damn. He hadn't meant for that to come out.

"Jack had plenty of good things to say about everything. After you left, we finally got around to talking about the college classes for credit. Like Patrick and the rest of our audience, Jack loved it."

Derek couldn't help a spark of pride from lighting up inside of him.

As Christina took a couple more steps into the room, he could see the flush of her skin intensifying.

Was she fighting it, too? Remembering the way she'd kissed him, held on to him, molded her body against his?

When she smiled softly and glanced at the carpet, he knew it was true. His heart banged against his rib cage.

Why? It didn't make sense. Maybe it was because Christina Mendoza was all contradictions: increasingly willing, yet a double dose of challenge that he wasn't used to.

"What're you working on now?" she asked.

"Getting started on the rooms."

"Not yet you aren't." She raised her voice. "Ready!"

A round of cheers sounded from outside his lobby and, through his windows, he could see the rest of the team—Twyla, Seth and Jonathan—enter, carrying a cake and beverages.

Finally, Christina brought her hands out from behind her back. Champagne glasses.

"To a job well done!" she said, beaming.

"Booze?"

"No." She guided Twyla and the cake to the table by the entrance. "Sparkling cider. We still have a lot of work to do today, so it's no use clouding our heads. Still, we deserve some good times."

As Seth and Jonathan poured, Twyla came over to pull Derek out of his seat. He thought he detected a curious glance from Christina as the blonde linked arms with him and led him to the treats.

But then his analyst glanced away and laughed at something Seth said, making Derek wonder if Christina cared about Twyla's flirtation at all.

In moments, they all had filled glasses raised in a toast.

"Boss?" Christina said, indicating that he should lead.

Boss. That told him all he needed to know.

Officially, the kiss had never happened.

Derek wasn't in the mood for toasts or celebrations. "Here's to Seth and Jonathan climbing on the Pecos College wagon and getting it up and running. Today. And here's to Twyla arranging in-house personal development classes. Starting now. And here's to me and Christina Mendoza putting together the next presentation. Pronto."

Elevating his glass, Derek quickly tossed back the cider.

Twyla, Seth and Jonathan just stared at each other, then cautiously consumed their own drinks. Christina merely tapped her fingertips against her glass.

"That's it?" she asked. "Not even a half hour to bask in a bit of glory?"

"I've got a lot to do."

Derek wanted to clam up, to stop his simmering resentment from ruining everyone else's day. In fact, he hated that his ego was so damned easily bruised.

Christina had tilted her head, gauging him with that clever gaze, as if she knew exactly what was bothering him.

"You were sensational," she said. "Every person in that room realized it."

"Enough."

Her eyes widened, lips parting ever so slightly.

Her compliments had pushed a button in him, revealing his need to be valued by Jack. The emotion made him weak, and seeing her acknowledge it laid him bare.

Even though a hidden, more logical part of him adored her for what she was trying to do.

As she lifted her chin and concentrated on drinking her cider, Derek wanted to say he was sorry, to brush his fingers over her temple and hold on to her.

But he was too strong to do that. Too mired in old habits.

While Seth cleared his throat and Jonathan shuffled his shoes, Twyla caught Derek's eye. She was sending him a saucy smile, just like the ones he'd caught all of last week.

But before Derek could discourage her with a stern glance again, a hearty laugh filled the outer lobby and he saw that Patrick was approaching. The old man had been at the presentation, nodding the whole time, offering his tacit support.

Derek's hero.

His former partner burst into the room, a bolt of welcome energy. "Here they are, the company's saviors!"

Immediately, the team's spirits rose. Dammit, Derek could take lessons from Patrick: Don't let your soft spots affect your attitude and get in the way of work. Always be encouraging.

As Christina hugged Patrick, laughing with him, Derek felt more alone than ever.

"Christina's right," Twyla said, having sauntered

over, as if sensing his isolation. "You're the best, Derek."

The way she said it, voice teasing, lashes lowered, made the New York Derek go, "Hmm. Gimme a Lite."

A woman like Twyla, with her one-inch skirts and three-inch heels, could banish his bad mood very easily.

But as Christina talked with his old partner, her words as bubbly as the sparkling cider, Derek realized that all his Lite cravings had gone flat.

Or maybe his fascination with this woman was just a phase, a hunger to have what seemed impossible.

Twyla was pulling on his sleeve suggestively, so Derek patted her shoulder in a professional manner, letting her know that he wasn't interested.

With a disbelieving arch of the brow, Twyla shrugged, then went back to the cake table to refill her cider glass.

Ten minutes later, after Patrick had flattered them all he could, the team vacated the room, promising Derek they were getting right back to work.

That left him with Christina and Patrick.

The older man grasped his protégé's shoulders. "I knew I made the right choice, asking you to turn this place on its head. You make me proud, son."

Derek couldn't hold back a swell of gratitude. "Thank you."

"Christina." Patrick kept one hand on Derek and

hugged her with the other arm. "Initially, I had no idea what a team you two would make. Now, the sky is the limit. You're both absolutely golden around here, and I'm not just talking about the opinions of the bigwigs. From the clerical assistants to the brokers, word has already gotten around about the programs. When I walk around the building, I can feel a change in the air. Excitement. Optimism. Something we were lacking before."

It looked as if Christina were about to walk on air. "You don't know how happy I am to hear that. Let's just hope this change is for the long term."

"I have no doubt of it." Patrick squeezed both their arms. "How about whooping it up with dinner tonight? My treat for such a stupendous job."

Derek glanced at Christina at the same time she checked out his reaction.

Dinner? she was probably thinking. Wouldn't that be too personal?

But how could she use that as an excuse when she'd laid one on him last night?

Seeing nothing untoward in the situation, Derek said, "I'm in."

Christina still hadn't answered.

"Come on," Patrick said to her. "Lacey will come. And we'll bring your folks, too. What do you think of that Brazilian steak house near the river?"

Obviously, the mention of other diners had put Christina more at ease. "Sounds great."

"Seven thirty, then." Patrick nodded, making the offer final.

"Gotcha." Christina gave him one last hug, then made her way toward the exit. "I'll need to get cracking if I'm going to accomplish anything today. Derek, I'll clean up the cake later. Patrick might want some."

Then she waved and left the room, Derek training a gaze on the way her hips swayed while she walked.

"Buddy boy." Patrick poked him in the ribs with an elbow, and Derek straightened up.

The old man had a curious gleam in his blue eyes. "Is that notorious Rockwell animal magnetism working on her?"

"Christina?" Derek shook his head, went back to his desk. "She's off-limits, Patrick. Look but don't touch. That's my motto with employees."

"Is that what you were saying when young Twyla was ready to puddle at your feet?"

Twyla? It took a second for her face to register over the lingering image of Christina.

"Listen," Derek said. "We're both guys. We know how we function. So maybe I've thought about Christina in ways that are…let's just say 'intriguing.' But that's as far as it goes."

Patrick didn't say anything for a second. "That'd be your loss, then. She's quite a woman. I guess some lucky man will find that out soon enough."

A shard of envy cut through Derek, but he didn't respond to the bait. Instead, he said, "So seven thirty, huh?"

Nodding with a grin, Patrick raised a hand in farewell. But not before he lobbed a final comment at his protégé.

"Work away, my boy. I hope it's enough to keep you warm at night."

Then he was gone, the observation leaving Derek cold.

The steak house was decorated like a rain forest, brimming with greenery, waterfalls and a Latin drum soundtrack. Waiters went from table to table, offering different varieties of meat that they carved right off their skewers: lamb, pork tenderloin, filet mignon, rib eye. This piecemeal method of eating was known as *churrascaria del rodizio*, derived from a time when cowboys used to barbecue their food over an open flame.

To Christina, it was food heaven.

And willpower hell.

Kind of like that kiss with Derek had been.

As she sat at the table with him, Lacey and Patrick Fortune and her own parents, she tried to keep her mind on family. The bet. Her work.

But it just wasn't happening.

Every time she took a sip of Syrah wine, the wet warmth of it would remind her of his lips, the spicy taste of him. She wanted to savor the memory, take it into her until she shivered with the heady feelings he'd evoked: Passion. The longing for the slide of his bare skin against hers. Acceptance.

But that last part had been real quick to evaporate. *Acceptance.* After all, when he'd ended the kiss, he'd acted as if it hadn't even happened.

Well, she'd taken the hint, wounded and maybe even relieved that he'd ignored her folly. And this morning at work, they'd gone about their business.

Best thing that could've happened, really. She'd gotten that one moment of impulsive desire out of her system, and she was all the better for it.

She was ready to forget and party the night away.

For the hundredth time, she concentrated on keeping her attention away from him and on her joyful companions. But it was so hard, with Derek sitting right next to her, freshly showered and wearing a smart button-down with khaki pants and Doc Martens.

She'd changed out of her office garb, too, choosing something more casual after her own shower. An herbal-scented body splash. Black underwear and bra. A sleeveless "little black dress" that was elegant, yet understated. Black pumps with straps decorating her ankles. An intricate black hair clip to hold back a loose chignon.

But even though she was wearing black, her insides were smoldering, still sizzling with longing.

When she'd arrived at the restaurant, Derek had been the only one at their reserved table, on time to the minute. He'd watched her walk to him, a feral flare in the way his gaze bathed her from her toes to her head.

"You look like Audrey Hepburn at a fiesta," he'd said, a ragged crack in his voice.

She'd wanted to cuddle against him right there and then, but she knew what sort of reaction she'd get.

More rejection in spite of the invitation. Who needed that?

Then, minutes later, Lacey and Patrick had arrived. The magnate's wife commanded the room with her cool grace, blond-gray hair swept back, green eyes connecting with Patrick's every other second, it seemed.

And then Mama and Papa had come through the door, dressed in sunset colors, raining kisses on their daughter when Patrick lavished more praise on her work.

They'd ordered wine, dined on meat and conversation, the hours passing like minutes. Even Christina, who normally didn't indulge or loosen up around business associates, found that the company and surroundings had liberated her even more.

Now, as they enjoyed after-dinner drinks and the restaurant crowd slimmed, the party still hadn't ended for their table.

"I have to admit that this is a fine eatery," said Jose, her distinguished papa who liked to dress in swanky suits. He was wearing one even now. "It doesn't compare to Red, but then, what does?"

Mama tweaked her husband's arm. "Your restaurant is the toast of Texas, *mi corazon*. You don't have to fish for compliments from us."

"Yes," said Christina, "even now I'm dying for one of Papa's wonderful margaritas. No one makes them like Red."

"Oh," he said, "you do make me conceited, Christina."

Derek raised his *caipirenha*, a drink similar to a margarita, but with the emphasis on lime.

"Here's to pride in a job well done," he said, "whether it be in Jose's restaurant, Patrick's businesses, Maria's knitting store, Lacey's charitable causes…"

He took a deep breath, making the table laugh as they proffered their glasses, too.

"…Christina's grace under pressure or my tendency to crack the whip too enthusiastically."

"Amen to that," added Christina, thinking of the day he'd dragged her away from the barbecue for the sake of work.

While they all clinked glasses and drank, Derek nudged her leg with his under the table.

She did it right back to him, carried away by the high spirits.

"Such a taskmaster," Patrick said, sounding tipsy and jolly as his voice bounced off the restaurant walls.

The sober Lacey put a finger to her lips. "Shhhh. Lower the volume on that megaphone."

Mama giggled, having consumed her share of wine.

Thank goodness they were all taking Patrick's

chauffeured Town Cars back home, Christina thought.

Patrick bussed his wife on the cheek. "Thank you, my darling." He started again, softer this time. "A taskmaster. That's what our Derek is. I saw that aura of success when I first laid eyes on the boy. I'm pleased to have been the one to discover him."

"I'm happy about it, too." Derek, who seemed more relaxed than usual, but hardly inebriated, was watching Patrick with great affection.

The emotion snuggled around Christina's heart.

"And I'll tell you this." Patrick leaned an elbow on the table, pointing a finger in the air, glasses slipping down on his nose. "He'll own the world in two years, give or take."

Lacey adjusted her husband's glasses, then caressed his cheek.

Mama balanced her arms on the table. "My Christina is quite the winner, as well. Did you know that she made the dean's list every year in college? And that she's received numerous awards from her employers?"

"I did," Patrick said, winking at Christina.

She flashed a smile back.

"Did *you* know," he added, "that Derek closed on one of the biggest business deals in New York history?"

"He's exaggerating," Derek said.

"Bigger than Donald Trump?" Jose asked, impressed.

Patrick looked secretive. "Let's just say Trump doesn't always work alone."

Papa gaped at Derek. He watched *The Apprentice* way too much.

"Bueno," Mama said, "but Christina won a big jogging marathon in L.A."

"Oh, stop," Christina said, laughing, even though she was embarrassed.

"We're so proud of both of you." Mama held a hand over her heart. "You two, with your ambition and drive, match each other in so many ways."

Ay.

Christina could sense Derek's gaze on her. But she wasn't going to look. One glance would break her down.

Don't do it, she thought. Don't…

She did.

Christina's blood started bubbling, fired up from the spark of their eye contact.

He was lifting an eyebrow, his grin indicating that he wasn't at all offended by her mother's runaway mouth.

Maybe he was even interested….

Nah. A relationship with Derek Rockwell? It could never work. And based on Christina's experience with bosses, she wasn't even willing to give it a chance.

Too bad, because with the way she was feeling tonight—after such a successful day—she was somewhat out of her mind, temporarily brave, willing to step out of her personal-space bubble and take a risk.

When Patrick started agreeing with Mama about the whole "perfect match" thing, Lacey whipped out her napkin and covered his mouth with it, wiping away the remnants of dinner.

"This one's got to catch his jet to New York in the morning," she said. "I think it's time to tuck him in to bed."

"Ooh la la," said Christina, the words slipping right out in the groove of the moment.

Everyone oohed and chuckled, causing Patrick to teasingly shake his finger at Christina.

Next thing they knew, Jose was noting that old people aren't equipped to party like the young. And, besides, they were the only ones left in the restaurant.

Grudgingly, all of them stood. Dinner had come to an end.

Patrick settled the bill, and they all thanked him, making their way out the door. Then the Town Cars pulled up, waiting for them as they said their goodbyes, Mama hugging Derek like one of the family before the vehicles drove them away.

That left Christina all alone with the boss.

Away from the office.

Going back to her condo seemed like a social death to her. The night was too beautiful. The dinner had been too uplifting.

Why did it have to end? she thought, not wanting to face another quiet night.

"You going to get home all right?" Derek asked.

In his more casual clothes, he seemed less intimidating, more like a man she could approach and talk to—if she normally did that sort of thing.

Before she could think about what she was saying, the words tumbled out.

"Actually, I was thinking of getting a drink."

He paused. "A drink?"

"Yeah." Oh, boy, what had she done? He was going to pretend she hadn't invited him anywhere, just as he'd done with that kiss. Ignoring the heat, the heavy breathing, the arduous contact of their bodies.

"I'm too hyper to go home," she added.

"You've really loosened up." He laughed, running a hand through his hair. What was next? A "Thanks, but no thanks"?

"I guess I'm still adrenalized. I only had one glass of wine all night, so it's not like I'm out to get tanked."

"Oh, I'm not saying you're drunk." He paused.

She steadied herself for the rejection. The hurt, just like she'd felt today in the office when she'd tried to compliment him about his performance.

"You have a place in mind?" he asked.

There was that grin again, aimed at her, ready to fire.

My, oh, my.

While her blood was busy pounding in her veins, she managed to nod. "There's a great bar about a block away, also by the riverfront."

"I'm game."

There was a growl lurking just beneath his words. What had she invited?

Whatever it was, the threat of being exposed excited her.

Christina, girl, she thought. What are you doing?

Having fun, said a side that rarely emerged. *Getting loose and enjoying life a little.*

"Come on then." She led the way, flashing him a shy smile.

And he followed, just as she'd hoped he would.

Chapter Seven

As Derek and Christina walked toward the river-front bar, his mind kept reeling.

Ms. Mendoza, frosty business analyst, had invited him for a drink.

First a kiss and now…

What the hell was happening?

He could hear the place before they actually arrived. Salsa music, with its driving rhythm woven through with percussion, piano and bass, mixed with the night air.

Bandini's. It almost looked like a shack floating on the San Antonio River, with red chile and white fairy lights shining over the low glow of fiery lanterns. Many of the rickety wooden seats were empty, but that was only because everyone was having a great time on the roomy, planked dance floor.

Christina, obviously moved by the steamy atmosphere, grabbed his hand and led him to the bar, where they each took a stool and ordered drinks. A margarita for her, a longneck beer flavored with lime for him.

Then they drank and watched the dancers: The women in their red dresses, gyrating, flirting. The men responding in a musical counterattack.

Leaning toward him, Christina spoke in his ear to be heard over the song. Her words tickled, warming him.

"See the couple in the upper right corner of the floor?"

Derek spied them, two particularly good dancers.

"They're here every time I come," she said. "Champions or something."

Bending over to talk in her ear, Derek caught a whiff of her hair's herbal fragrance, the perfume of her skin. He shuddered, getting used to taking her in.

"There are such things as salsa competitions?"

When she maneuvered her mouth near his ear again, he turned his head to accommodate her, but not soon enough. Her lips brushed his cheek, and she drew back, laughing at the unexpected contact.

Even though her mouth had left a burning imprint on his skin, he couldn't help laughing, too, connected to her by the awkward, incidental touch. Back in the office, this would've been a big deal. But here, in a salsa bar with the moonlight and music, it was more of an icebreaker.

A peek into how happy they could make each other if they'd both let down their defenses for a night.

And that's *all* it'd be, he told himself. A night.

Never anything more.

She tried again to speak into his ear, this time bracing a hand on his shoulder. Her touch was light, enough to hammer his pulse.

"Competitions are what some of these people live for," she said.

Before she could move away, Derek took a chance, cradled the back of her head with his hand, kept her in place. All he had to do was turn his face to speak into her ear.

Some of her hair had come loose during the course of the night. This time when he talked, his breath moved a few of those strands. They caressed his face, adding further heat to his yearning for this woman.

"You must come here a lot," he said.

She didn't move from their intimate pose. Encouraged, he trailed his fingertips from the back of her head to the side of her neck—casual, but not demanding. Once there, he rested his thumb in the moist dip separating her collarbone, his fingers coming to linger in the crook of her neck and shoulder.

He thought he heard her breath catch.

"I come by every so often," she said. "I live close. And they serve good enchiladas here. Amazingly healthy."

So she wasn't a barfly. That was no surprise. But still, Derek could detect a loneliness similar to someone who sat drinking, waiting for a stranger's company night after night.

He lightly coaxed his thumb up the center of her throat, and she swayed in her seat, anchoring an open hand on his thigh. Longing tightened his belly.

"Did you really bring me here for a drink, Christina?"

When she didn't answer, he coasted his hand upward, using his thumb and forefinger to frame her chin. Guiding her face toward him, he met her gaze.

Hazel eyes, dark in the low, red light. Liquid in the way they were asking him to keep touching her.

He traced her full lower lip, entranced by its softness, and she closed her eyes.

This couldn't be happening, Christina thought.

Sure, she'd invited him here for a drink, but she'd been warring with the don't-do-it chiding of her common sense the entire way.

Now, as he caressed her mouth with his thumb, the long-dormant desire to be loved again crushed her barriers, told her it was all right to give in.

Just a little.

Hesitating, she parted her lips, allowed the tip of his thumb inside her mouth, where she sucked, then let him loose.

A sense of pure delight consumed her. Oh, that had been a bad-girl move. And it was addictive.

But she shouldn't go any further, not even an inch more.

The seductive gesture had Derek reaching out with his free hand to take a fistful of her skirt.

"Do you know what you're doing to me?" he asked.

Encouraging you to kiss me again, she thought. *And to have you admit that you want me this time.*

A slow, sexy song came on, the volume waning, the pace of the dancing slowing to a hush. Waves of motion from undulating bodies both calmed the room and turned up the temperature at the same time.

The feverish heat was getting to her. That had to be it. Why else would she be asking herself if she could manage to get back at him—even a little—for rejecting her?

At the same time, why shouldn't she be the kind of woman who danced under the spell of salsa, just as she'd wanted to for so many late, quiet nights while she'd sat at a corner table eating dinner and watching all the couples?

Holding her breath, Christina pulled Derek off his stool. He followed her to the floor.

She turned to him and started a more deliberate version of the dance she'd been doing last night in the deserted conference room, right before the kiss. Swirling her hips, shoulders. Smiling at the freedom of losing herself in the seductive tempo.

Through her eyelashes, she saw him standing

there, watching, an obvious hunger building up in the clench of his fists, the quickened pace of his breathing.

Tell me you don't want to kiss me again, she thought.

Taking both of his hands, Christina imitated what she'd seen the dancers do a thousand times, arranging his palms on her waist, then sliding them down to her hips.

Oh, this felt right. And it would never have to be mentioned again between them. Not if she stopped in a few more decadent seconds.

But that's clearly not what he had in mind.

With a ruthless grin, Derek took over, pulling her flush against his body, letting her feel his arousal, the wicked effect she had on him.

As she opened her mouth, he eased his palms from her hips downward, smoothing over her rear end. Then, with a semirough thrust upward, he pressed her into him.

Time to stop now? asked her brain.

Hell, no, said her traitorous body.

Eyes wide, she bit her lip, locking gazes with him, doubting the wisdom of what she'd conjured in Derek. She'd gone too far, hadn't she?

Not that she was really regretting it. But she should be.

Really. She should be.

But, somehow, she wasn't.

He leaned down, mouth to her ear, to talk over

the music. Every warm word drained more strength from her.

"I'm tired of ignoring what's going on between us," he said. "It's there, like it or not."

Game over. She'd proven her point, right? He was primed for a kiss—and more.

It would be smart to walk away now, get back to the land of personal bubbles and private spaces.

While she was arguing with herself, his hands traveled up the lines of her back, melding her to him. He positioned one palm on her hip, while the other hand held her fingers.

A more traditional slow dance style.

Christina's blood gave a *za-room!* Fluid electricity flashed through her veins, numbing her to any thought of leaving.

But she didn't want to anyway. Didn't want to stop what she'd started.

How long had it been since she'd last felt like a woman?

Too long. And she didn't want to give it up.

For a full minute, they ignored the music, moving in time to their own sensuous song. Gradually, she nestled closer to him, lost in the found comfort of his arms.

"Have you ever had an affair with a co-worker, Christina?" His voice was hoarse, graveled.

"Not an affair."

Would one night with Derek qualify? Would it get her in as much trouble as the rumor of sex had with

William Dugan? Granted, she'd been innocent in that scenario, but…

Was being with the boss a wise move?

Did she even care at this point?

And what about that dating bet she had with her sisters, the one that was based on men being nothing but trouble?

If she stole a teeny bit of breathless serenity from Derek for just one night, would it matter? Would she lose for winning?

"What did you have if it wasn't an affair?" he asked, words stirring aside her hair.

With her free hand, she rubbed up and down his biceps, testing, enjoying.

"It was nothing," she said, not wanting to remember Dugan.

Then, proving to herself that she could carry on with a normal love life, even after what her old boss had put her through, she ran her hand upward, spanning the back of Derek's head, drawing him down to her lips once again and taking control of the situation.

Her choice this time. Not Dugan's. Not Rebecca Waters's.

This kiss was softer than the last one, a lazy, searing promise of what could be.

So good. Salt, lime and beer.

With building passion, Derek increased the pressure, parting her lips with his tongue, meeting hers with easy strokes.

They'd stopped pretending to dance altogether, unable to help themselves. She was getting dizzier, each step convincing her more and more that she could get away with one full night of bad judgment.

But then a new song came on, fast, loud, frenzied.

As a whole, the crowd cheered, whipped into a flurry of motion.

The two of them merely came up for air, lips still poised against each other as they struggled to breathe.

Then she stood on her toes again, snuggled her mouth against his ear.

"What would happen if you came home with me?"

Du-du-du-duuuuuh.

She couldn't even believe she'd said it.

"You know the answer, Christina. Think about what you're asking for."

She had. Believe it.

And even though she knew this was wrong, she wanted him. Body and soul, this would sustain her. Maybe even change her life.

As an answer, she snuggled against his chest, unwilling to give him up for principles.

That's when he grabbed Christina's hand, made quick work of paying the bartender and brought her outside.

From there, she guided him to her condo, which was only minutes away.

It wasn't long before she was fumbling with her keys and crashing open her door.

This was *muy loco*. Yet good. Oh, very good.

But it'd been so long, she thought, practically yanking Derek inside her home, stumbling backward as the weight of him crashed into her.

"Whoa," he said, regaining his balance, holding her against his chest as he braced a hand against the tiles of her foyer wall.

With the other hand, he shut the door, the sound making her realize that the way back to yesterday was sealed off.

Whenever they looked at each other in the office from now on, they'd know. Their bodies would no longer be secrets. Their souls would be laid bare tonight.

And Christina was ready for it.

She started to unbutton his shirt, fingers trembling.

Would she remember how to have sex? Would she be terrible at it? After all, her last boyfriend had been Carson, and that was five, long, pathetic years ago.

Derek laughed low in his throat, the mirth rumbling through his chest under her hands.

"Wait, sweetheart, wait." He shifted position, backing her against the wall to stare up at him.

See, she'd already done something wrong. Too eager.

Ease up.

"I just want to…" He hesitated, then touched her hair.

An Important Message from the Editors

Dear Reader,

If you'd enjoy reading romance novels with larger print that's easier on your eyes, let us send you TWO FREE HARLEQUIN SUPERROMANCE® NOVELS in our NEW LARGER-PRINT EDITION. These books are complete and unabridged, but the type is set about 25% bigger to make it easier to read. Look inside for an actual-size sample.

By the way, you'll also get a surprise gift with your two free books!

Pam Powers

Peel off Seal and

Place Inside...

LARGER-PRINT
FREE BOOKS
EDITION

THE RIGHT WOMAN

she'd thought she was fine. It took Daniel's words and Brooke's question to make her realize she was far from a full recovery.

She'd made a start with her sister's help and she intended to go forward now. Sarah felt as if she'd been living in a darkened room and some- one had suddenly opened a door, letting in the fresh air and sunshine. She could feel its warmth slowly seeping into the coldest part of her. The feeling was liberating. She realized it was only a small step and she had a long way to go, but she was ready to face life again with Serena and her family behind her.

All too soon, they were saying goodbye and Sarah experienced a moment of sadness for all the years she and Serena had missed. But they had each other now and that's what

She held

Printed in the U.S.A.
Publisher acknowledges the copyright holder of the excerpt from this individual work as follows:
THE RIGHT WOMAN Copyright © 2004 by Linda Warren. All rights reserved.
® and TM are trademarks owned and used by the trademark owner and/or its licensee.

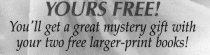

The Harlequin Reader Service™ — Here's How It Works:

Accepting your 2 free Harlequin Superromance® books and gift places you under no obligation to buy anything. You may keep the books and gift and return the shipping statement marked "cancel." If you do not cancel, about a month later we'll send you 6 additional Harlequin Superromance larger-print books and bill you just $4.94 each in the U.S., or $5.49 each in Canada, plus 25¢ shipping & handling per book and applicable taxes if any.* That's the complete price and — compared to cover prices of $5.75 each in the U.S. and $6.75 each in Canada — it's quite a bargain! You may cancel at any time, but if you choose to continue, every month we'll send you 6 more books, which you may either purchase at the discount price or return to us and cancel your subscription.

*Terms and prices subject to change without notice. Sales tax applicable in N.Y. Canadian residents will be charged applicable provincial taxes and GST.

If offer card is missing write to: Harlequin Reader Service, 3010 Walden Ave., P.O. Box 1867, Buffalo, NY 14240-1867

BUSINESS REPLY MAIL
FIRST-CLASS MAIL   PERMIT NO. 717-003   BUFFALO, NY

POSTAGE WILL BE PAID BY ADDRESSEE

HARLEQUIN READER SERVICE
3010 WALDEN AVE
PO BOX 1867
BUFFALO NY 14240-9952

NO POSTAGE
NECESSARY
IF MAILED
IN THE
UNITED STATES

A drift of moonlight from the windows revealed a look of tender longing on his face.

Or was she projecting what she felt onto him?

Slowly, he undid the clip holding up her chignon. As her hair unfurled to her shoulders, he dug his fingers into it, playing with the strands, leaning forward to take in the scent of it.

"You never wear it down," he said. "Drives me ape because I've always wondered what it looks like."

As he nuzzled against her neck, Christina sunk into him, wanting to feel herself against his hard body.

Tentatively, she started to unbutton his shirt again, delving her hands under the material, grooving her fingers into the muscled ridges of his abs, his ribs. Gliding her hands upward, thumbs catching the crests of his nipples, she circled over them until he groaned.

Shivering, she reveled in the power.

She could turn a man on.

Derek caught her lips with his, his hands roaming her hair, her neck, her shoulders.

When they stroked downward to cup her breasts, Christina leaned her head back, thrilling to the play of his fingers, the sensitivity of her arousal.

"You're melting," he said teasingly, talking against her throat. "The first day you walked into my office, I wanted to do so many things to you…"

"Like what?" she whispered, stimulated by the thought of him fantasizing about her.

Just as she had about him, night after night.

He reached around to the back of her dress and, as he undid it, the zipper sounded like a descent of sorts.

Her fall from the throne of an ice queen.

"Like this." He eased the material away from her shoulders, kissing her skin in the wake of it, grabbing a hold of one bra strap with his teeth and leading it down her arm.

He inserted a thumb beneath the other strap, stripping it off, also. The black lace seemed to disappear as he then unhooked the bra.

That left her standing there, knees weak, breasts exposed to the night air. To his gaze.

With maddening care, he licked at one nipple, drew around it with his tongue. Then he surged forward, taking it into his mouth to suck on it. He paid close attention to the other one, too, cupping her breast in his palm, kneading it gently.

Arching up to meet him, Christina worked his shirt off, craving the feel of his skin, which was damp with a thin sheen of sweat by now. She ran her nails over his back, moving her hips in time to the laving of his tongue.

A humid steam was building up in her, making her ache and grow more restless. She wiggled her hips, sliding down the wall a fraction, unable to stand on her own anymore.

He laid her down on the lush carpet, kissing his way down her stomach, tugging at her dress, turning his body sideways so he could coax the linen over her legs and strappy shoes.

Stroking her lower belly, he glanced up, a wild gleam in his dark eyes. She gave a frustrated little cry, his hands so close to where she really wanted them to be.

"And what else did you want to do to me?" She was panting, hardly even sounding like her normal self.

He caressed the length of one of her legs, then parted them so she was open for him.

Bending down to her kneecap, he spoke against it. "I want to turn you to water."

Por favor. Please, please, please do.

Trailing his mouth up her inner thigh, he nipped his way to the center of her.

On the edge and even somewhat anxious, Christina shifted. She'd positioned her arms over her head, seeking something to grab onto. As she found a wrought-iron table leg, she held on for dear life.

He'd moved his body between her legs, maneuvering one over his bare shoulder, causing her pump's heel to scratch against his back.

"My shoes…"

"No," he said, rubbing his clean-shaven cheek against her thigh, "leave them on."

Part of his fantasy?

Then he nudged the center of her, her panties wet, telling him how ready she was. Gasping at the contact, Christina lifted her back off the carpet to meet his mouth.

While he loved her through the lace, she rocked with every kiss, her breath coming in tiny pants.

One of her hands came to rest over her eyes, the other clutching the table leg. She could hear the terra-cotta plant vase on top of the table jerking back and forth with her exertions. Without really knowing what she was saying, a stream of Spanish words tumbled out of her mouth.

Faintly, she was aware of him removing her underwear. She was too busy climbing to greater heights to notice much else.

Her vision was caving in, swirled with the red of salsa lights, the sparkle of water under a night sky. Stars pulsated, coming in and out of focus.

Boom. Ba-boom.

As he increased the pace of his intimate kisses, her heart almost fluttered apart, almost disconnected into pieces that would be floated away by her simmering blood.

"Derek," she said, not really intending to say anything. Not knowing what to say. "Oh…"

The stars in her blurred sight winked, beating in a chaotic frenzy. Flashing. Bursting. Showering all over the sky and dropping to water with the hiss of a beautiful death.

Lungs burning from her frantic efforts at breathing—or had she been holding her breath?—she clawed for air.

But Derek was unforgiving, gliding up her sweat-slicked body, pressing his chest to hers, devouring her mouth in a famished kiss. Possessing her.

Catching his fever, Christina grappled with his belt, got it loose, undid his pants and got them off with his help. They managed to get a condom out of his wallet at the same time, then opened the wrapping.

He was hard against her leg. Greedily, she reached down, stroking the condom over him.

"There are so many things I want to do to you," she said in a whisper.

"We've got lots of time until sunrise."

As he looked down at her, his short brown hair ruffled by her fingers, sweat beading his forehead, Christina thought she detected a splinter of feeling in his eyes. A fleeting admission that they'd have to face more than carpet burn by the start of tomorrow's work day.

He smoothed away a strand of wet hair that had stuck to her forehead, traced his thumb over her cheekbone. "You do something to me, Christina."

For a moment, there were no more words. Just lulling caresses. Just the two of them.

Then he seemed to realize his honest admission and recovered with a slow grin.

The gesture caged her, reminded her of his abundant charm and all the doubts she'd had about it. His was the smile of a confirmed bachelor. A sidestep away from the emotion she'd seen on his face only a second before.

But they'd gone too far for it to matter. She'd made her decision to be with him and she'd have to deal with the consequences.

Because it'd sure been worth it so far.

Reaching down, he slid his fingers between her legs, opened her for him, then slipped inside of her, filling her up until she had to bite into his shoulder to ease the new, yet old, feeling.

He must've felt her tightness, because he paused.

But she took up where he left off, grinding against him, wanting more.

What started as a slow dance built into a faster, more intense tempo. Since she hadn't yet come all the way down from her last orgasm—wouldn't it be nice if she never did?—she was halfway to crying out his name already.

As he drove into her, she moved with him, needing to take him all in, to savor every second of this high-flying ecstasy.

In this new world, she shot back up to the stars, touching the sizzling core of them, becoming part of the light, basking in their glow.

Then she flew to another, and another, brushing too close to the heat, the burn, the sweet agony…

Downward again, back to earth, wings melted and—

Crash.

An explosion, tearing her apart.

As she embraced him, her skin prickled with heat, rivulets of sweat running to the floor. The weight of him made her dizzy but, still, she held him close.

Wondering what would happen when sunrise came.

Chapter Eight

Afterward, Derek tried to seem as unaffected as possible, removing her shoes and tickling her feet, carrying her to the bedroom so they could spend the rest of the night there.

Christina had just thrown him for a loop, that's all. Come morning, she'd be out of his system. If they were lucky, Derek could even turn this experience to their advantage, erasing the tension between them, relaxing all the "what-ifs" and returning their main focus to business.

That's what he told himself, at least, as he watched Christina snooze once again.

As with the other night in the office, she was sleeping the slumber of the innocent.

Earlier, she'd turned on a dim lamp at his request, allowing him to enjoy every inch of her beautiful body as they made love a second time. Now, with her dark hair spread over the pillow, her face smooth, her hands cupped near her chin, he could hardly believe this angel was the same woman he'd made love with an hour ago.

But, hell, it wasn't much of a shock to Derek that she matched him in passion—he'd been banking on it.

In his experience, in fact, it was always the prim and proper types who turned up the most heat.

But not as much as Christina had.

The way she'd cried out his name…the way she'd bitten his shoulder during the throes of climax…

"So can we manage each other tomorrow?" he whispered now, skimming a finger down the elegant slope of her nose.

Her only answer was a deep inhalation, a satiated "Mmm" as she stirred and resumed her regular breathing pattern.

Truthfully, lingering in a woman's bed was a new experience for him. Too bad he hadn't explained his usual type of "date" to Christina before they'd come back to her place. When he'd promised to stay until sunrise, he hadn't been thinking clearly.

Still, he didn't feel all that compelled to leave just yet.

In all honesty, he could even sit here, listening to her sleep, until morning. There was something sublimely intimate about it, as if he were awake to protect her during the most vulnerable state of existence.

Guardian of her slumber, he thought.

Overcome, Derek bent down, gently nuzzled the tip of his nose against hers.

Okay, wait.

Derek backed away. Had he just been Eskimo-kissing a woman?

With a sneaking sense of doom, he moved to the other side of the bed.

The snuggle had been rash. He hadn't meant it.

Especially since it was something Sir would've done, back when Mom was alive. Back when she'd been lying in that hospital bed when he'd finally come home from that dirt-poor Third World hole where he'd been stationed.

In fact, Sir *had* done the Eskimo kiss on Mom, avoiding all the tubes attached to her arms, leaning over her sleeping form, rubbing his nose against hers. At the same time, a tear had fallen from that hard bastard's face and onto her pale skin.

"Please don't die," the old man had said in a softer version of his Southern-fried bark. "Stay."

He obviously hadn't known that Derek was awake and when he'd sensed his son's awareness, there'd been hell to pay. Sir always needed to take out his disappointments on someone, and Derek was always pretty convenient for that.

Dammit, he thought, trying to brush away the

memory. Wasn't there a cigarette or something around here that could buzz the pain away?

Then again, he didn't smoke. Too unhealthy. But maybe he should pick up the habit, just for moments like this.

At a loss, Derek fidgeted, wondering if slipping out of Christina's bed without saying goodbye would be considered bad form.

She stirred, stretched. "Time for work?"

Her voice was no more than a slurred mumble. When he glanced at his lover, she resembled an awakening kitten, fuzzed by slumber and too much warm milk.

Here was his chance. He could thank her for a great night, explain his philosophy of noncommitment, then sweet-talk her into feeling good about herself anyway.

But he'd never encountered a Christina before. She wasn't Lite. Wasn't someone he could so easily lead or dismiss.

Derek didn't stop to think about why that was.

"We still have hours left," he said, wanting to touch her so badly, yet not daring to. "Go back to sleep."

Coward.

"Want something to eat?" Christina struggled up, holding the sheet over her breasts, hair a cloud of dark brown silk.

"Only if you have potato chips," he said, joking around. He knew full well that a health nut like her wouldn't have any junk food on hand.

She looked guilty.

Laughing, Derek said, "You're kidding. What're you doing with bad eats in your house, Christina?"

"I didn't say I had some."

"You didn't have to." Quite naturally, he was back to feeling comfortable with her. "Be honest."

"Oh, boy…" She leaned her head on the cushioned headboard and scrunched up her face in defeat. "I've got a few chips around. Just crumbs, though."

"Really. So if I got out of bed and went to your cupboards…"

He made a move to do just that, and she grabbed his arm.

"All right, you caught me. I'm a food pig."

An image of her slim, rosy-skinned body, coated by a silver veil of moonlit sweat, crashed over him. Hers was not the figure of someone who snacked on too much fatty grub.

"You could've fooled me," he said, relaxing and sliding to a cozier position where he could lean on an elbow.

Hey, shouldn't he be going? Wasn't that what his conscience was telling him to do?

Now, it told him. *Go go go—*

Yet…he wasn't moving.

At least, not in the way he should've been.

Instead, he found himself reaching out to her half of the sheet, lifting it to peek underneath.

She swatted it down, laughing. "What are you doing?"

"Enjoying every moment." Until what they had together needed to end.

Then he took a different tack, avoiding her reach by slipping his hand under an opening near her knee.

"Derek!"

Grabbing onto her, he squeezed, making her jump.

"Calm down," he said.

"I'm calm."

But she giggled, telling him she was nervous about something.

A bout of threatened tickling?

Probably not.

How things would work out in the office tomorrow?

More than likely.

He started to stroke her thigh. "Shhh. See, I mean no harm at all."

"You? Derek Rockwell?" She settled down under his soothing caresses, raised an eyebrow. "I think your self-perception differs from that of everyone else's."

"Tell me then. What does the rest of the world think about me?"

As his hand crept higher, she slumped lower, her bones seeming to soften.

"About you? Well, I can only say what *I* think."

"Go on."

He massaged her upper thigh, and Christina closed her eyes, lost in his ministrations. Her blushed skin fascinated him, made him feel good about making *her* feel good.

"From what I've heard and the little I've seen,"

she said, "you're a heck of a businessman. Great instincts. Wonderful head for numbers. Calculating in the way you go after what you want."

Calculating.

It sounded too much like someone else he knew—cold, precise, demanding.

"Is that how I come off?" he asked, trying to act like it didn't matter.

"You don't appreciate the description? People work for years to establish such a business reputation."

Had he spent so much time trying to avoid being like his father that he'd accidentally morphed into him?

No. Sir had never indulged in a careless good time. Not with women, not with life. He wasn't a risk taker.

Derek was his *own* man.

Taking his hand away from Christina's thigh, he said, "I'm not just talking about my professional appearance."

His voice had been too quiet. Great, why not bare all his fears to her?

Christina gauged him once again, sympathy in her gaze. She scooted over, coming face-to-face with him as she leaned her elbow on the mattress and rested her head in her palm, too.

"The truth?" she asked.

"Sure."

"Out of the office," she said, "you're just as fantastic."

Derek tried to shut out the voices of the other women who'd cooed to him in bed. Somehow, he'd been born with the gift of knowing how to talk a smooth game, how to touch them in the right places and leave them happy.

But that was all superficial, because he had no idea how to truly love anyone.

And he was beginning to think that Christina deserved so much more.

Hesitantly, she brushed her fingertips against his upper chest, playing with a few hairs.

"You don't have to answer this, but…" She paused, smiled. "I'm just curious about a superstar like you. Does a tycoon generally have time for girlfriends?"

Here came the pillow talk. Was she trying to get a feel for how far tonight would extend into their daily lives?

Since he'd failed to establish his boundaries with her before, now was as good a time as any to make the situation clear.

"I don't have a lot of time for dating, no."

"Me, either. I tell everyone I'm in love with my career." Her laugh was forced. "Being good at corporate dealings sure makes it tough to put anything—or anyone—else first, doesn't it?"

"You're right." She seemed to be doing all the work for him, laying down reasons for why this night would be their only one together.

While relief flooded him, regret did, also.

"So," she asked, "have you ever had any time in your busy schedule to fall in love?"

Now was the time to tell her.

"Come to think of it, I've never told a woman I've loved her."

He'd meant it to sound like a gentle warning, but instead, the confession shook him to the core.

Even Christina's eyes told him how damned sad it was.

"Never?" she asked, as if giving him a chance to amend his answer.

"Never. I don't do well in relationships."

"Oh." She removed her hand from his chest, laid it on the mattress.

Already he missed the contact.

After a pause, something seemed to kick in with Christina, a realization.

When she shrugged good-naturedly, Derek lost hope, lost the fleeting thought that maybe a woman like Christina would have the power to turn him around.

Right.

"Actually," she said, "I don't do so well, either. In relationships, I mean. I guess I've always been too driven to put a lot of effort into men, much to Mama's dissatisfaction."

Derek wished he still had a mother who was alive enough to give her opinions about his lack-of-love life. "You're telling me that guys aren't beating down your door?"

She seemed taken aback. "Of course not."

Huh? Didn't she know what a knockout she was? Or was Christina Mendoza one of those women who couldn't believe the best about themselves?

Inconceivable.

He wanted to tell her that any man would be fortunate to win her love. That she should have confidence in what a great catch she was.

But he could hardly say those things when he wasn't willing to go any further with her.

"Hey." He ran a forefinger under her chin, flicking it, flirting. "I feel lucky to be with you tonight."

It was the best he could do without seeming like a fraud.

"Thank you," she said, brightening a bit.

They both smiled at each other, and she went back to touching his chest.

That was better.

"I could live with your compliments," she said, not meeting his gaze. "It's an improvement over being called 'cold' or 'removed.'"

Derek frowned. "Someone said that to you?"

"Oh, my first real boyfriend, actually. I was a late bloomer, always more into my books than I was boys, so I didn't really begin a social life until college."

"Don't worry. This fellow Army brat I knew when I was a kid acted the same way. And he was a guy. In high school, he took this personal oath that'd he'd make love only with the woman he married. That, of course, changed during his freshman year of college, but you're not alone, Christina."

"Good to hear." She crept closer to him, inserting a long leg between his own. "I never really minded my atypical dating behavior. As Mama always said, I was too independent to care—and too shy. Besides, I got my kicks from good grades and academic competitions, not sorority socials."

Derek absently ran his knuckles over her arm, watching the fine hairs rise off her skin. "And when did that end?"

"Sophomore year. The first bloom of amour."

"Young love," he said, sort of wishing he had a story or two to tell her.

No chance of that. Derek had spent the tender years of dating in much the same way as he had his adult life—short, to the point, then bye-bye. In truth, he'd moved to so many Army bases that Derek hadn't been given the opportunity to develop many relationships, but that wasn't much of an excuse.

"Well, my love story doesn't exactly have a happy ending," she said. "My boyfriend got frustrated with me and my ambitions after a mere two months, then told me that—let's all say it together—I was…"

She tapped Derek's collarbone while she said the words. "Too cold and devoted to my work."

He wasn't about to tell her that he'd had the same impression until recently.

"After that," she continued, tone studiously flippant, "I went into Christina World, where it was all about moving up the ladder of success."

"And you did pretty damned well."

She didn't respond, only bit her lip.

To get her attention again, Derek tugged at the sheet, exposing the swell of her breasts. The sight was like a punch to his gut.

But a nice one.

"So he was your only boyfriend?" he asked. "Ever?"

"Seriously?" She swallowed as he pulled the sheet all the way down to her waist. "There was one more. Didn't end well, either. Lots of misunderstandings, because I thought he was more into my sister Gloria than me."

"Then he's a fool." Derek's voice was choked with lust as he scanned her body—the small, but full breasts. The tiny waist and flat belly. The slender, toned hips. The endless runner's legs.

He must be a fool, too, he thought.

Probably able to read every wolfish thought in his mind and body, she casually covered herself with her hands. When she spoke, her voice was resigned, yet not unhappy.

"I've learned a lot of lessons from those fools, Derek. When I was younger, I had so many pure ideals that I clung to—things I was taught by my family, my community. Then I got older, and waiting for love didn't seem to make much sense anymore. I don't expect much from men now."

He averted his gaze from her, thinking he was a

letch for wanting to love her again after her frank admission.

"As a matter of fact," she added, laughing a little, "I've got a bet going with my sisters. None of us is supposed to date for a whole year. I thought it wouldn't be a problem."

He could detect the question in her words: had she lost the bet by being with him?

As he was thinking about the answer, she sighed, came to rest against him, body-to-body, holding him to her.

"But this definitely does not count," she said, "me and you being together for one night. I'm off the hook if you don't spread the word."

A thread of relief snapped inside of him but, at the same time, he couldn't help feeling disappointed.

So she'd never expected more of him than this, he thought. A one-time fling. Christina was as obsessed with business as he was, and their tryst wasn't anything more than it seemed.

She'd gone to great lengths to explain this.

"You promised me the sunrise," she whispered, then pressed her lips to his neck, kissing her way downward.

And he took Christina's loving for what it was worth: a single night of sheer bliss.

She woke up alone the next morning to the ding of her doorbell.

Groggy from lack of sleep, Christina practically

rolled out of bed, wincing at the soreness of muscles she hadn't used in years.

After blinking herself awake and glancing at the clock—shoot, she'd forgotten to set her alarm and it was a half hour after her usual reporting time—Christina absorbed the sight of her rumpled bed.

The evidence of Derek having slept there last night.

The word *sleep* being debatable, of course.

Was he still here in the condo somewhere?

Two more dings echoed through the air. Maybe it was Derek?

Christina smiled, a false sense of modesty causing her to grab a white terry-cloth housecoat, then stumble to the door.

Their sex-a-thon must have made him as famished as she was. Maybe he'd decided to surprise her with coffee and hot buttered corn tortillas from the café next door?

And to think she'd believed that she'd scared him off for a minute there last night. When he'd asked about old boyfriends, she'd only wanted to make light of her very thin book of love. Had wanted to put Derek at ease, since he'd seemed so out of sorts, slumped against the headrest on his side of the bed.

But she'd also wanted to test the waters, she supposed, dancing around the subject of relationships. Seeing if one could possibly be in the cards for them.

Then she'd started thinking that bringing him

home had been a mistake. And that's when she'd told him about the bet.

As she'd hoped, the mention of it had relaxed him, brought them back to the lighthearted love-making she'd relished earlier in the night.

In the end, part of her celebrated the fact that he'd wanted her passionately and that the rejected kiss hadn't been any indication of her unattractiveness.

His body had told her just how beautiful she was.

Still, another part of her wondered why she wasn't enough woman to keep him for more than a night.

The bell dinged three times.

But maybe he was here right now, asking to come back in.

Trying not to seem too excited, Christina whipped open the door, letting in the early-morning light.

And there stood Mama with her new friend, Edith.

"Rise and shine!" she said, bustling past her daughter while dragging Edith in behind her. "We were having breakfast at La Tapatia down the street when we decided to catch you before you went in to work."

Sure. And the sky was actually made of blue cotton candy.

At least Derek wasn't here. That would've been a definite nightmare, not to mention a slight technicality as far as the bet with her sisters went. But she and Derek weren't really *dating*. Not if his quick disappearing act had anything to do with it.

"I invited Maria to dine with me this morning," Edith said, as if the excuse were scripted.

A thin, nervous woman with black hair, she worked at Fortune-Rockwell as a broker's assistant. About a month ago, Patrick had suggested that Edith check out Mama's knitting store in Red Rock, seeing as his employee was an avid craftswoman herself. She and Mama had hit it off, scheduling breakfast every week in San Antonio.

They'd just never stopped by Christina's apartment before.

"Welcome, Edith," Christina said, not wanting to be rude. "Something to drink?"

She'd just stay later at work to make up for the time she was away from it now.

"No, we are all coffee-ed out," Mama said. "I wanted Edith to see your pretty place, is all."

With that, she started to play tour guide, pointing out Christina's Southwestern flair for decorating, the wooden statues of saints, the Mexican pottery and frozen sun motif in the pictures and sculptures.

In the meantime, Christina waited, highly suspicious of this visit.

Her worst fears were realized after Mama's token five-minute excursion had ended.

"You had some fine times last night," she said, Edith following quietly in her shadow. "How did everything turn out, *mi hija?*"

"Whatever do you mean, Mama?" Christina widened her eyes at her mother in exasperation.

"I mean you and Derek were the only ones left after dinner."

Even Edith seemed interested. But of course she was. As sweet as she seemed, she was one of the biggest gossips at Fortune-Rockwell. Luckily, Christina had managed to avoid the yap-yap trap so far, thank goodness.

"What?" Christina said. "Two grown people can't stand on a sidewalk together at night?"

"You do not like him?" Mama asked. "I do. For my bookish daughter, it will take an aggressive man to pull her out of that shell she is in."

"Maybe your judgment was affected by too many drinks?" Christina asked.

"What a way to talk to your Mama." The matron patted her dark, gray-streaked hair in patent pride. "Besides, I can hold my liquor."

Edith piped up. "Derek is a favorite with all the ladies, so I'm not surprised you like him, Christina."

Newsflash: Women liked Derek. Details at eleven.

"Oh, yes," Mama said. "Patrick has mentioned the parties and the socialites in New York. But we can all turn over a new leaf. Besides, he is *muy guapo*, yes, Christina?"

Something Derek had said last night about never falling in love came back to haunt Christina's doubts.

"He's a womanizer, all right," Edith added, "but you just can't help adoring the man. It's like his smile's a hook and, if you don't want to get caught, you'd better get out of the way when he flashes it. All the women in administration talk about his cute butt."

"How many of those women has he dated?" asked Mama, all territorial-like.

Good, because Christina was wondering the same thing.

"Oh, he doesn't date in the office. Not as far as I know, anyway. If he does, he keeps it quiet."

Gulp. Was that what Christina had been? A secret that would be notched in his memory?

Her heart sank. She'd made a mistake, hadn't she? What had she been thinking by sleeping with her boss in a moment of mind-scrambled yearning?

Hadn't she learned anything from the past about how sex and business can't mix?

What would she do if things fell apart at the office?

Dumb, dumb, dumb.

"Excuse me," she said to Mama and Edith. "I've got to get ready for work. And for the last time, I'm not interested in Rockwell. Do you understand?"

Mama sighed, resigned. "Then we'll be going."

She came over to squeeze Christina, reemphasizing to her daughter that there would always be family.

Even if business failed.

After Edith said her farewells, they left Christina to a quick shower.

That's when her mind started to whir.

He's a womanizer, all right. His smile's a hook.

And he hadn't been in bed to greet her this morning.

Dios, maybe Derek Rockwell was even laughing

at his desk right now, congratulating himself on conquering the office ice queen.

She'd taken a chance with a man who'd made no promises to her. All of the blame for her discomfort rested on her shoulders, and that made her so very angry.

Angry at herself for losing her head.

No more. From now on, it was business only. Even if his words were charming. Even if she couldn't forget how his kisses branded her, revealing her passion, restoring her confidence, just for a night.

She had to take control of the situation now.

As Christina left her condo, her determination grew with every mile that closed between her and the office.

There was absolutely no way she'd allow her life to fall apart because of a boss again.

Because once had been enough.

Chapter Nine

At sunrise, Derek had quietly gone straight from Christina's condo to his place near the river. There, he'd prepared his rowing equipment and taken out his frustrations on the misty water, slicing through it, obliterating it with each dip of his oars.

But he hadn't exorcised his demons.

In fact, he'd been even angrier at himself after he'd showered and come into work before most people had even finished their morning cup of coffee.

As he paced his office floor while trying to read a financial report, questions kept running through Derek's head.

Why hadn't he stayed with Christina until she'd woken up? Or why hadn't he even left her a note?

Maybe it was because of how the dawn had bathed Christina's body as he'd awakened. Or maybe it was because of how her gorgeous, turn-your-heart-upside-down face looked, so peaceful and happy.

When he'd laid eyes on her first thing this morning, emotions he couldn't identify—didn't *want* to identify—had attacked him, taken him down like lightning slamming into a tree.

And Derek had panicked, remembering the bet Christina had talked about.

The one that told him he was expendable.

Confused and rattled, he'd left her to slumber, needing time to be away from the temptation of her.

Needing time to get it together.

He was still in the process of doing just that when she showed up in his office, an hour and a half late for work.

Not sure how to interact with her, Derek tossed the report on his desk. It gave him something to do, especially during this initial moment of morning-after awkwardness.

"I know," she said, "I'm late. It won't happen again."

After coolly sauntering to a chair, she sat and crossed her legs. Her earth-colored skirt suit covered most of what Derek had enjoyed last night. And if *that* didn't hint that things were definitely back to business as usual, her upswept hair practically shouted the message.

As did her aloof attitude.

First things first, he had to apologize for this

morning, even though his mind told him it'd been the right way to handle this delicate situation.

"Christina, before the rest of the team gets here, I want to—"

She held up a hand, silencing him, shooting him a detached smile. "That isn't necessary. What happened last night, stays in last night. Know what I mean?"

A slap in the face would've been more comforting. At least, then, he would have known that she cared.

"I'm going to have a hard time forgetting about our time together," he said.

Dammit, that hadn't been the right combination of words at all.

"You...what?" she asked. "I thought..."

She stood from the chair, calmly walking toward his attached suite.

When she saw that he wasn't following her, she made a subtle motion with her hand.

Come in here.

Might as well get this over with.

She led him to his walk-in closet, then waited in front of a row of hanging suits, arms crossed over her chest.

As soon as Derek entered, Christina explained *her* rules, words tinged with a thick, emotional Spanish accent.

"To be clear, last night can be filed under the category of Unmentionable. It was a mistake. A momentary loss of brain power."

It was as if a blast of freezing air had whisked through Derek's body.

How could she be so cold about what they'd shared?

Or had their connection—the touching of two lost people—been completely one-sided?

Hell, no. She'd returned every kiss, measure for measure. Derek hadn't been imagining it.

"A mistake?" he asked. "You know better, Christina."

She bunched her fists, but was still collected. "I wasn't thinking clearly, and you... Even *you* don't fish in the office pool."

"True. But even though this makes business somewhat more challenging, we didn't make a mistake."

After he said it, he realized it was the truth. He wouldn't take back their lovemaking for anything.

How could she not feel the same way?

Now his dander was up. "Do you want to pretend nothing ever happened?"

He thought he saw a burst of pain in her gaze.

"That would be a good idea," she said. "We could go back to square one and—"

Without thinking, he stepped closer to her. In reaction, she backed up, hangers clanging as she mashed into his suits.

Her reaction baffled him. "Christina...?"

What was going on? On the one hand, she was watching him with the same look he'd seen last night: eyes soft and willing, lips parted.

But then again, she had a hand in front of her chest, palm out, as if posting a barrier between them.

"This is not a good idea," she whispered.

She hadn't told him to get lost. Hadn't told him that he was overstepping his bounds.

Were her words more of a warning to herself than to him?

Slowly, he took her hand, massaged it with his thumb, gentling her.

"Just tell me you still need me," he said.

"I will not."

Her breath was coming in tiny gasps as she stared at the floor. But she hadn't told him to stop touching her. The minute she did, he'd back away, give up, admit that last night *had* been the world's biggest error.

Encouraged, he turned up the steam, using his other hand to caress the underside of her jaw.

Her eyes fluttered shut, and her hand started to tremble.

"Tell me last night was no fluke, Christina."

"I won't do that."

And she meant it, she thought. Their time together had changed everything—office dynamics, the way she saw the world.

The way she saw herself.

It hadn't been a negative experience. *Dios*, in fact, Christina wanted much, much more. Her body craved him as if he were a forbidden opiate, one that made her feel sexy, dreamy, content.

Even now, as his fingertips danced over her throat,

warming her deep inside, she wanted to cast aside all her doubts and promises from this morning. Wanted to tear off both of their clothes so they could meld together again.

"Derek…" she said, trying to put him off, but knowing her heart wasn't in it.

He must have taken his whispered name as an invitation, because he pressed his lips against her forehead. A red-hot, moist sear of possession, marking her.

"Say it, Christina." He spoke against her skin, just as he'd done last night against her knee, her thighs.

The memory of their joining tore her apart: the building tension, blinding heat, shuddering ecstasy.

He'd owned her, body and soul. But at this moment, the two halves were warring with each other for dominance.

Her body said: *Derek wants Christina, and Christina wants Derek. Why fight it?*

But this isn't based on any real emotion, said her soul. *It won't ever be love.*

Then her brain kicked in, reminding her of Edith's words this morning: *he's just a womanizer.*

And she'd allowed him to be one by inviting him into her bedroom.

Why did all those mixed thoughts have to remind her of William Dugan and the trouble he'd caused her?

As Derek cupped her face in his hands, brushing her cheeks with the pads of his thumbs, Christina gathered all her strength.

All her experience.

"It was a mistake," she repeated, latching onto his hands with her own, removing them from her skin.

Obviously frustrated, he clenched his jaw.

Cold air took the place of his touch on her skin, but Christina told herself she didn't mind. She was doing what was right. Protecting herself in so many ways he'd never understand.

He backed up, clearing the way for her to leave the wardrobe area ahead of him.

"I won't mention it again," he said stiffly.

With every step she took away from him, her heart cracked a little, like ice forming over what was once fluid and open.

And, when she reached the office and took a seat, waiting for the team to arrive, she couldn't help feeling as if she'd returned to a throne.

Whether she wanted it or not, the ice queen was back.

By lunchtime, Twyla was crying.

Dammit, Derek hadn't meant to bring her to the point of tears. But she'd been so busy being precious, making an impression on their two additional team members—Adam and Ben—that she was failing to concentrate. To brainstorm different components of a "creative room" where employees could go to relax and reenergize at the same time.

"Twyla," he'd said to the blonde after the third time she'd made an irrelevant comment while dimpling at the male team members, "stop messing around and earn your paycheck."

Right off the bat, he knew she'd been more embarrassed than anything else. But it'd taken a few seconds for her tears to drop from her face, down to the notepad paper she'd come to stare at.

"Aw, jeez," he'd said, ticked at himself.

Maybe he'd still been stinging from Christina's rejection this morning and that was reflected in the demands he was putting on the team. But one thing he knew for certain was that they were going to produce another fabulous presentation, come hell, high water or even Twyla's tears.

Her flirting would only distract them.

With a chastising glance at Derek—yeah, he deserved it for being so snappish—Christina had led an upset Twyla into the wardrobe suite.

The place seemed to be a hot spot for controversy today.

As the males—the returning Jonathan and Seth, plus the two new guys—all sat around and cleared their throats, Derek was thankful that he and Christina were still able to work well together.

Yes, they were civil and productive. But simmering underneath every verbal exchange, every glance, was the knowledge that he'd been inside her. That he'd explored every inch of her body.

Good God, it was hard to keep his mind on anything else.

After a few minutes, Christina and Twyla re-emerged, the young assistant much too reserved.

Had Christina seconded Derek's opinions about keeping the flirting out of the office?

Damn, he felt like a hypocrite. And to make matters worse, his act of wounding Twyla brought back bitter memories of his father and what he used to do to Mom and Derek with his verbal abuse.

Well, Sir and his harshly precise lifestyle could go to the big military base down below, for all Derek was concerned.

Maybe the old man had even ended up there.

"I think this is a good time to break for lunch," Derek said.

"I'm heading for the cafeteria," Twyla said much too quickly.

Without wasting a second, she darted out of the room, followed by the guys.

As Christina gathered some papers, Derek couldn't help thinking she was staying behind for a good reason.

"Go ahead," he said. "Let me have it."

Pausing, she glanced up at him, all traces of the passionate woman he'd known last night gone.

"Twyla's still inexperienced and kind of hormonal, but she's a good worker. She didn't mean to put a kink in your well-oiled machine of corporate progress."

Why was there an echo beneath every one of her words?

We made a mistake, a mistake, a mistake…

"I need everyone on track," he said, ignoring the reminders.

She finished putting away her papers. "Why? Do you have something to prove?"

"To who?"

He came around to the front of his desk, his body vibrating like a damned divining rod in her presence.

She put her hands on her hips, as if girding herself against him. "Jack, that's who. Just because you two are vying for the position of Number One Son with Patrick, don't drag the rest of us into it."

"That's bull," he said, knowing she was all too right.

"Is it?"

He really didn't need a lecture, especially from a woman who'd messed with his mind enough already.

Needing a breather, he walked past her. "I'm going to put some diesel into my engine."

And he was out the door before she could say anything else.

Fine timing. Not only could he escape the frustrating enigma that was Christina, but he could grab something to quench his dry mouth. And while he was there, he could even meet his apology quota for the day and say sorry to Twyla.

As he headed for the cafeteria via the elevator, he tried to keep his head from exploding.

Jack. The presentation. The maddening woman who'd turned his world topsy-turvy in the matter of a few days.

What had happened to the carefree life he'd shaped for himself?

After searching for the break area—this was only the second time he'd been there aside from a first-day tour given by Patrick—Derek asked directions from a female broker. She seemed stunned that he was talking to her.

Excellent. Nothing like being the boss everyone cringed from. He'd taken great pains in New York to avoid that sort of reputation, and he'd have to correct it.

When he got to the crowded lunchroom, he acclimated himself, remembering how the place was set up. Vending machines were located in a far alcove, where a few more tables waited, allowing some privacy for the workers.

Walking through the hamburger-and-grease-tainted room, he left a trail of hushed conversations in his wake, all the while searching for Twyla. When he stopped to ask a table of women if they'd seen her, they accommodated him by pointing to a room just behind the soda machines.

Efficient. He'd get his drink, then drop in to do a little employee maintenance.

As he deposited his coins into the slots, he heard whispers from the nearby tables, then a discussion from around the corner. Sounded like Twyla's voice, but she was hidden by half of a wall, and Derek couldn't be sure.

"…and then she told me that flirting in the office would get me in a sticky situation," she said.

Definitely Twyla's chirpy twang.

A male voice—Adam?—said, "If you ask me, I'd follow Christina's advice. You just never know these days. As a guy, I'm scared to death to tell a harmless joke for fear that some woman's going to jump all over my case. It could mean a sexual harassment suit."

Derek's ears perked up with interest.

"Oh, lighten up," Twyla said. "When I smile at you during work hours, do you feel threatened? That's all I was doing."

Several male voices laughed and denied the danger to their manhood.

Derek knew he shouldn't be here listening, but he was still trying to decide which drink he wanted. Water or Gatorade? Decisions, decisions.

Besides, they were talking about Christina. How could he not be lured by the subject?

"At any rate," Twyla continued, "she's the last one to talk. I heard through the grapevine that she was out with Derek last night. *Out* out, if you know what I mean."

What? How did they…?

"Are you sure?" It sounded like Seth, a stalwart kid if Derek had ever met one. "Christina's a pretty straight arrow. All business."

"Oh, yeah." Twyla laughed. "Edith Lavery was at Ms. Monkey Business's condo this morning, and she thought something was brewing between our boss man and Christina. Something more than just flirting. I mean, how dare she lecture me about office etiquette when she boinks her way into jobs?"

Hoooold on. Enough was enough.

As the guys at the table responded by either questioning or protesting, Derek stepped around the corner to indeed find Twyla holding court in a near-empty alcove with a kitchen sink and refrigerator. Seth and Jonathan had already stood from their seats.

All of the crowd blanched when they spotted him.

"For the record," Derek said, voice barely held in check, "Christina Mendoza is qualified beyond a doubt. And gossiping about your bosses in the building is probably not the wisest career move."

"I...uh..." Twyla said.

"Stay here for a minute, Ms. Daraway. For the rest of you, take lunch somewhere else. And I suggest you come back to my office in forty-five minutes with your minds erased of idle gossip."

"Yes, Mr. Rockwell," the guys said, filing past him with lunch trays in hand.

As Seth and Jonathan walked out of the room, Derek nodded to them, knowing they weren't the cancer in the group.

That left Twyla alone with him.

"Care to explain why you'd stab Christina— who's only looked out for you from day one—in the back?" he asked.

"I didn't mean anything by it." Twyla's face was

red as she locked her gaze on the table. "It's just that I heard—"

"Do you realize what gossip could do to a career?"

Especially a woman's, he thought, regretting that he'd inadvertently made this happen to Christina.

He was no stranger to the female mind. He knew how ruthless they could be when it came to taking each other down. Part of him couldn't help wondering if Twyla was jealous of the rumored romance since *she'd* been trying to win him over herself.

"I didn't realize…" she said, just about shriveling into her bright blue suit.

"This is the way it works," Derek said. "We're going to Personnel, and they'll counsel you about spreading malicious gossip. It'll be documented and serve as a warning."

"But…"

"Listen, Twyla. Christina's on your side. We both agree that you're a strong employee, but we don't play turncoat here at Fortune-Rockwell. You need to adjust your attitude if you want to be here for the long run."

Drawing herself up, Twyla raised her chin. "I'll stop. I promise, Mr. Rockwell."

Should he believe her? As Christina had noted, this woman was still young and would make many mistakes in her career. Hell, he'd been the same way, even under Patrick's guidance.

Truthfully, Twyla seemed to have the stuff of success in her, and maybe that would win out over her missteps.

Still, what she'd said about Christina made him want to stand up for his employee, to defend her.

But his outrage was purely professional, he told himself.

"On a personal note," he said, anger boiling over once again, "I respect Ms. Mendoza more than you can imagine. She's an amazing businesswoman, and she doesn't deserve your pettiness."

"I really am sorry." And Twyla looked it, with her mouth turned down in a frown and her lashes batting furiously to keep back more tears. "I'll apologize to Christina and tell everyone that the rumors aren't true."

"That's a start," he said.

As he waited for his employee to walk out of the room ahead of him, Derek finally chose water from the vending machine.

He'd need something to put out the flames he'd caused for Christina.

"She said what?" Christina asked, feeling the blood drain out of her skin.

Derek had dismissed the team to work on individual projects for the afternoon, asking his right-hand woman to stay behind. But she'd had no idea he was going to tell her about Twyla and her lethal gabbing.

Sitting her down on the leather couch—probably because it looked as if she were going to fall—Derek said, "Twyla was telling the guys about a rumor that's going around. Your mom's friend, Edith, has been talking."

This wasn't happening. Not again.

Years ago, Rebecca Waters had done the same thing to Christina. Had told the entire office that she was bringing sexual harassment charges against William Dugan for no good reason. That Christina had tried to seduce *him* and had become resentful when the married William had spurned her advances.

Derek glanced at his assistant who was planted just outside the door at her desk. He'd made sure Dora would be present during this entire talk, just so they wouldn't be alone anymore, causing additional gossip.

"Twyla won't do it again," he said, "not after she realizes how serious this is. Personnel is taking care of that right now."

"When I was twenty-four," Christina said, "I wouldn't have dreamed of talking that way about my boss. Do you think this was all an innocent error? Or does she have an agenda?"

When Derek didn't answer right away, Christina shook her head, then asked, "Are we keeping Twyla on the team?"

"I'm leaving that up to you."

After everything that had happened between them, it was nice to know that he still respected her judgment.

"She's doing a bang-up job with the classes," she said. "Taking her off that project would set us back."

"Then maybe we can leave her with that and use the guys for the new phase. That'll give Twyla the opportunity to show us she's serious about making some amends."

"Sounds like a good solution."

But what was she going to do about Edith? The older woman couldn't help herself when it came to flapping her jaws. Maybe Christina should invite her to breakfast tomorrow along with Mama, just to let them know how much damage had been done.

Derek was watching her, concern etched in the tiny crinkles near his eyes. His gaze had darkened, black as a deep cave that hid thousands of secrets.

Was he angry because his employees had misbehaved today?

Or… Christina didn't even dare think it.

But she did. Was he enraged for her sake?

Something told her it was more personal than business, that he was offended for her. The realization warmed her frozen heart, made her feel protected, even though he was the one she needed to guard against.

"Christina," he asked softly, "are you okay?"

"I'm just fine." She couldn't let him see how Twyla had reached in and stirred awake her worst fears.

"All right, then." This was his cue to go back to his spot behind the desk, but he didn't move. Instead, he reached one of his hands toward her, as if he wanted to touch her again.

Wounded by today's events, Christina jerked back from him, eyes wide.

They both stared at each other, at a loss.

An eternal second later, she jolted out of her seat and gathered her materials. "I'll be in my office."

Blocking out his response, she didn't look back at him.

Because all she'd see was her past.

And *all* of her mistakes.

Chapter Ten

Christina managed to get through the rest of the week without more professional disasters.

Though the gossip hadn't wrecked her career, it had made her a minor celebrity of sorts around the office. Wherever she went, gazes followed, and she knew what they were probably thinking: *She's sleeping her way to the top.*

But no one ever came right out and said it, due to the way Derek had handled Twyla and Edith, whom he'd also sent to Personnel for counseling and paperwork.

In truth, many employees acted as if they hadn't heard the gossip at all. A lot of them had even introduced themselves, thanking Christina for all her suggested company improvements. Thanking her for caring.

And, adding to the growing love train, Twyla had done her part by bringing Christina flowers while apologizing profusely for what she'd done.

As for the boss himself? Well, he'd taken to treating her like an official co-worker, never requesting one-on-one meetings without another person present. Never asking her to the corner café for lunch or dinner anymore.

There was definitely a professional distance between them, one Christina had encouraged herself.

But there were also moments that told her she hadn't gotten far enough away from him.

During every meeting, when she'd inevitably give in to the lure of glancing at her sexy boss—just to tide herself over, naturally—she'd catch him watching her with a breath-stealing hunger in his eyes.

But it wasn't anything more than lust, Christina told herself each time they'd lock gazes, then abruptly disconnect. By his own admission, Rockwell wasn't capable of anything more.

When the weekend finally arrived, Christina made a valiant effort to put the office behind her. Unlike the first rushed presentation, the team had this one well in hand. They'd be sharing their "creative" and "recreational" room findings late next week and, unbelievably, they were ahead of schedule.

Which meant she was allowed to enjoy herself for now.

If she could remember how.

At the moment, she was trying to do so as she sat at a courtyard table in Papa's restaurant, Red.

Relax, she thought, twisting a napkin in her hands.

Yes, *twisting*. Just like a heroine in a melodrama who was watching the mustachioed villain rip up the deed to her beloved land.

Realizing her failure to de-stress, Christina tossed the linen onto her lap and continued waiting for Gloria and Sierra to arrive for lunch. Papa had already been by to serve her a large, unsweetened glass of iced tea, garnished with a mint sprig and lemon, leaving her alone to listen to the burbling fountain as well as the never-ending Greek chorus of her conscience.

She wasn't going to think about Fortune-Rockwell anymore, darn it.

Instead, she reminded herself of how lucky she was to be back in Red Rock. And in Red itself.

The restaurant was a converted two-story hacienda that had once been owned by a historically influential Spanish family. While the first floor was decorated like a cozy *casa* with thick, dark-wooded tables and chairs, low lighting, greenery, ceiling fans and terra-cotta tiles, the second was used for office space and storage.

Though the inside was comfortable, Christina far preferred the courtyard. With the red umbrellas covering pine tables and gaily hued paper lanterns strung around the perimeter, she couldn't help but feel welcome here.

Just as Christina finally closed her eyes and permitted herself to do nothing for the afternoon, Gloria arrived, placing a hand over her sister's mouth.

"Shhh," she said. "Something's going on."

When Christina opened her eyes, Gloria removed her hand, pointing toward the ivy-strewn iron gates that offered a peek of the outside world.

She could barely see two people standing there, facing each other. Voices murmured, words unintelligible.

"It's Sierra," whispered Gloria. "And she's with one of her buddies. Alex Calloway."

"Oh, I've heard that name before. He's a friend from college, right? And she thinks he's always on her case."

"*Si*, Christina. You sound as suspicious as I am. Do you think he's a good way for Sierra to lose our bet?"

The bet.

Christina gulped. She wasn't going to say a word about losing it. Besides, she wasn't *involved with* Derek. Never had been.

That meant she was still in the race. Right?

As Gloria sat down, the sun shining on her long, honey-light hair, Christina saw that she was wearing a smart white halter top and skirt with new earrings. Graceful dream catchers, woven with turquoise and fine strands of silver.

Her sister's talent with jewelry choked Christina up a little. Yes, it was silly, to be emotionally moved by earrings. But this particular art had been Gloria's saving grace, a therapeutic way of recovering from alcoholism during her time in rehab.

She was so proud of Gloria for beating her troubles.

As Christina basked in the feeling, they both tried to hear what Sierra and Alex were saying to each other. But there were only raised voices, then a parting of the ways as the couple cleared the gate.

Alex went one direction, Sierra the other.

It didn't take long for their youngest sister to make her way to the table, a slight breeze knocking around the dark curls of her hair, the skirt of her pink sundress. She looked fresh, sweet, so baby-sisterish that Christina just wanted to protectively banish that frown marring her pretty face.

As they all hugged and kissed hello, Christina tried to ignore how out of place she felt in her conservative shorts and blouse. She was a soccer mom next to fashionable Gloria and lovely Sierra.

Think it's time to loosen up? she thought.

After all, it'd felt pretty good the other night with Derek.

"Sierra, what's wrong?" Gloria asked as they all took their seats again.

"Ohhhh." Sierra growled in frustration. "That Alex. You'd think I'd broken into his home or something with the way he treats me."

Christina and Gloria exchanged glances, knowing better.

"Are you caught up in his business?" Gloria asked.

"Of course not!" Sierra furrowed her brow, reconsidering. "Then again, maybe I was. But all I did was ask him if he'd purchased a gift for his adoptive mom's birthday yet."

Since Sierra had already told her sisters about her circle of college friends, Christina knew that Alex was touchy about having been adopted. Sierra's habit of tracking his personal relationships no doubt rankled him.

Christina wanted to comfort her younger sister, especially since Sierra had tried to make her feel better so many times in the past. She'd been one of few beacons of hope during the dark times of William Dugan and the falling-out with Gloria.

But, then again, all this worrying about other people wasn't doing Sierra any good. Christina hated to see her wilt from too much stress.

"Sierra," she said, placing a hand over her sister's, "even though you're so good at loving, you don't need to be everyone's caretaker."

After a pause, Sierra grabbed onto Christina's hand in a tender squeeze, then let go. "Maybe you're right. Maybe I won't give a hoot about Alex anymore. He doesn't appreciate my efforts anyway."

Leaning back in her chair, Gloria had a wheels-are-turnin' look in her eyes. "By all means, Sierra, please *give* a hoot. I have a lot of heinous work in mind. Lots of embarrassing chores to make up for your man temptation."

Oh, boy. Christina was in *mucho* trouble if they ever found out about Derek.

"No, oh, no." Sierra sat back, too, gripping the arms of her pine wood chair. "You won't see me losing this bet, Gloria. Especially not with a rude ingrate like Alex."

"That's all she wrote, then." Gloria turned her attention to Christina. "I guess I'll just have to depend on my big sister to blow it with Mr. Rockwell."

A mix of panic and shame led Christina to blush furiously. Panic because she didn't want them to know how thoroughly she'd lost the bet already. Shame because she didn't like keeping it from her sisters.

"I told you about last week's office gossip," she said to divert the guilt. "Rockwell is nothing to joke about."

"Oh, no jokes here." Gloria grinned. "The rumors, as unfortunate as they are, go to show that *everyone*—not only our family—has noticed the va-va-voom between you and the boss."

"Gloria," Sierra said, "you're just as bad as the gossips. Mama is angry with Edith because of the lies she spread. You don't want to be on her bad side, too."

"No, I sure don't."

Gloria seemed to shudder, just as much as Christina had when Sierra had mentioned the word *lies*.

Although Edith had been gossiping, she hadn't literally been lying about Christina's liaison with Derek. Thus, during breakfast a few days ago, Christina had gone easy on her, merely asking her to think about the effect her rumors had on other people.

But Mama hadn't been so forgiving. Even now, she wouldn't take Edith's calls, even though Christina was trying to convince her to forgive and forget.

Papa had walked into the courtyard, dressed in a silk button-down and dapper slacks. "Have my girls decided what I should cook for them?"

"Are you open for lunch yet?" asked Sierra. "We can wait."

"For you," Papa said, bending down to pat Sierra's cheek, "I'm always open."

"Aw, Papa," they said, standing, showering affection on him. After happily withstanding the onslaught of their attention, he took their orders: chicken tostada with no sour cream or guacamole for Christina, beef fajitas for Sierra and shrimp soft tacos for Gloria.

Before Papa left, he grasped Gloria's hand, inspecting it. "You are keeping a surprise from your sisters?"

Gloria actually giggled. "I'm getting around to revealing it."

"What?" Sierra asked. "What're you hiding?"

Papa stayed, and Christina guessed Gloria's news was something big.

"Tell us!" she said.

With a huge smile, Gloria reached into her purse, then slipped a beautiful diamond ring onto her finger.

Both Christina and Sierra gasped, then cried out, hugging their sister. Papa joined in but, when Christina detected a soulful tear in his eye, he retreated to the kitchen, muttering something about making tortillas.

While they all admired the ring, Gloria told them about how Jack had proposed. "He came to Mama and Papa late last night and asked them for my hand. Can you believe that? Jack, the gruff, stubborn manly man?"

"When's the wedding?" Christina asked.

"We're planning a small one for June."

"Oh!" Sierra's lower lip trembled, even though she was smiling. "I'm just so…so *happy* for you, Gloria."

Before anyone could react, Sierra darted out of her chair to crush Gloria in another hug, then ran into the restaurant.

"It's Chad," Christina said. "She still isn't over that jerk, but she's truly excited for you."

"I know." Gloria looked worried. "Do you think we should go after her?"

"In a second. Give her some time to recover. She'll be mortified about breaking down like this." Spellbound, Christina touched the ring. "Jack's one lucky man."

"Thanks. I just wish…"

"That Sierra and I would find men, too? Don't worry. There're other ways to be happy."

Leaning forward, Gloria took Christina's face in her hands, really looking at her. "You're going through something, aren't you? Maybe it has to do with all those stupid office rumors. Or maybe…it's more."

"It's nothing."

Her sister shook her head. "Don't fib to me.

Just…whatever it is, will you just follow your heart? I would have wasted much less time and trouble with Jack if I'd let myself trust and love a little easier."

Christina wanted to ask how Gloria was so certain this was about love, but she was afraid to. She was probably wearing her repressed emotions on her buttoned sleeve without knowing it.

There was a pause, weighed down with unspoken thoughts and explanations, but it was interrupted by the harplike ring of Christina's cell phone.

Gloria stood, gestured to the restaurant. "I'll check on Sierra."

"Be right there."

Alone, she allowed it to ring once more before she finally glanced at the calling screen.

Derek. The man she'd been dreading…and hoping…would be on the line.

Follow your heart, Gloria had said.

And, though it was so hard, Christina decided to try. She answered his weekend call.

After lunch, Christina went home to change into something more colorful: yellow shorts, a yellow-and-white-striped tank top and white Skechers. Then she'd pulled her hair into a casual ponytail instead of the librarian-like chignon she'd been favoring lately.

What could she say? Maybe she was in the mood for some change.

As she drove downriver, where Derek's condo

was located, Christina wondered if following her heart meant ignoring her brain.

Could I talk to you? he'd said over the phone. *I'd like to clear something up before office hours. If you feel okay about coming to my place, you'll be well chaperoned and no one will ever know you were here.*

She'd agreed, wondering what he'd meant by "chaperoned," but feeling secure about trusting herself around him if they were under observation.

And, let's face it, she thought. She'd seize any excuse to be around the guy.

When she arrived at the white, Mediterranean-style complex, she followed his directions, which led her down flagstone paths lined with man-made rocky streams. Finally, after passing blooming flower gardens and a variety of home security warning signs, she came to his slightly opened door.

The gaping invitation, in turn, beckoned her into a stately, yet modestly decorated condo exploding with a strange, dangerous buzzing noise.

She stuck her head around the door, knocking, calling out, "Hello?"

"Back here." It was Derek's voice, vying with that electronic sound.

Shutting the door, she ventured inside. A lemony scent tinged the air, as if the sleek, black furnishings had been recently polished to a shine. Extra rooms revealed the skeletons of sparse furniture, plus exercise equipment, including a rowing machine.

Interesting, how Derek didn't flaunt his great wealth. He could have afforded limousines, but instead drove his own Beemer. He could have lived in a mansion, but chose something more down-to-earth instead.

As she wandered closer to the noise, she noticed a wider selection of those primitive musical instruments that barely decorated his office: rawhide-bound drums, delicately painted stringed instruments, wooden flutes, a smooth rainstick.

Some of the items weren't even placed in strategic corners or hung on the white walls; a few were tossed over the beige carpet, used and abused.

The trail of instruments led to a state-of-the-art big-screen TV that showed two Jedi Knights in heated battle, their light sabers zooming across the screen in streaks of color. In front of the set were two hypnotized people, madly manipulating their control pads.

Derek and a young boy, who didn't look more than eight years old, with his spiky red hair and glasses.

Was this their chaperone?

"Glad you could come over," Derek said glancing away from the action.

He was dressed in a white T-shirt, faded jeans and work boots, his casual air lending him a ruggedness she'd never seen before. Even his hair seemed a bit longer, more carefree.

His lighthearted grin invited her to smile back,

and Christina couldn't stop her heart from twisting, wringing out any doubts she'd had about being here.

He had that expression on his face that guys usually got when they wanted to tell you how nice you looked—not that Christina had heard, or paid attention to, many of those. But she knew he wouldn't say it out loud, taking a chance on making her uncomfortable after all that'd gone on this past week.

Besides, she was wearing shorts. A ponytail.

She had to be misinterpreting the appreciative look in his eyes.

Derek seemed to have forgotten about the game, thus allowing his Jedi to get tossed across the space port by a flick of his opponent's hand.

"Hey," he said to the boy, "that's dirty."

"Of The Force, always be mindful." The boy laughed, then glanced at Christina. "Is she here to play?"

"You wish. I'm not about to subject her to your Dark Side." Derek pressed a button and set his remote on the carpet, then stood. "This is my guest, Richie. Her name's Christina Mendoza."

Getting serious, the boy got to his feet, too, then came over to shake Christina's hand.

"You wanna be a Jedi, Miss Mendoza?"

Shoot, yes, she would. This was some setup.

Derek interrupted. "We've got to do a bit of boring adult talk, so why don't you ask the computer to play against you and we'll be right outside."

Then, nodding to some rattan chairs on the jasmine-lined patio, Derek went to the fridge and poured them both some bottled water over ice.

Christina really would've liked to play, but now wasn't the time. "Good to meet you, Richie," she said as the boy went back to saving the galaxy.

"You, too, Miss Mendoza."

She met Derek on the porch, and he offered her the sweating drink. Richie was within sight, though the sliding glass door had been pulled to block out sound from both directions.

"Sorry," he said, indicating the water, "it's all I have. Time to do some grocery shopping."

"Water's perfect." She took a sip, then asked, "So, Richie?"

"A neighbor's son. He gets pretty lonely because his mom's out most of the time. I'm the baby-sitter of choice, I suppose."

"You?"

"Don't be shocked. I need an excuse to play video games, and Richie's it."

Touched by his obvious lie, Christina knew it'd be smart not to show it. So she glanced over the low wall, at the shimmer of the river as it lazily flowed by. "This is a lovely complex. Does she have to work as much as we do to maintain residence?"

"No, her ex-husband's loaded, and he pays for them to live here. For now, at least. She dates a lot. Looking for the second Mr. Right of her life."

Had Richie's mom given Derek a shot yet? Something told Christina that he'd probably taken one look at the young boy then removed himself from consideration. Just because he was a good baby-sitter didn't mean Derek the Womanizer was on the market for an instant family.

"She's on a first date as we speak," Derek said. "Who knows? Maybe this'll be her lucky day."

After he chugged some of his water, he narrowed his eyes. They'd darkened in the last few seconds.

"Are you angry about something?" Christina asked.

"Nah. Just…" As he cut himself off by closing his mouth, a muscle twitched in his jaw.

She leaned forward. "What?"

"It's… I guess I kind of feel sorry for the kid. Real sorry. Even though I haven't lived here very long, the father's barely dropped by. Two times in two months for visitation. Nice, huh? And I could hear some heavy yelling through the walls…Mom and Dad's happy reunion. The dad's a winner, all right, and I wish Richie didn't have to suffer for it."

Derek was tracing the rim of his glass with a fin-ger, avoiding her gaze. Condensation beaded on his fingertips, a drop falling to the concrete like a re-leased tear.

There was definitely something else going on here, Christina thought. A buried sadness. A jagged secret deep inside.

Through the window, Richie played on, one of Derek's instruments sitting near his leg. A rainstick.

Christina knew how they worked: turn them upside down and the broken pieces hidden inside trickled downward, creating soft, haunting music.

She glanced back at Derek, finding him watching her intensely.

Shaken, she fixed her eyes on the instrument again.

He must have followed her gaze. "Oh, yeah. Richie's new toys. My mom used to make my dad buy them for me, hoping to bring out this mysterious musical gene her side of the family was supposed to have. I got them out of storage because Richie likes them."

"They look foreign."

"I was an Army brat, so my father got around." The sentence was short, to the point.

"Do you still see your parents?"

Derek shifted in his chair. "Both passed away a long time ago. Hepatitis, then heart failure."

Before she could say she was sorry, a change came over him, a straightening of his posture. A return to control.

The boss.

"I didn't call you over to chat exactly," he said.

"That's right. Business." The avoidance of anything that mattered.

So why did she sound resentful? Wasn't that how she wanted it with him? Impersonal?

His arched eyebrow told her he was wondering the same thing. But there was no doubt he knew better than to ask.

"I was worried about you last week," he said.

"I told you, I'm fine."

"No, I meant…" He was searching for words. "How you reacted after I told you about Twyla's gossip. It concerned me. So I did some digging, Christina."

Her pulse started to pound. "What do you mean?"

"The charges." His voice was so gentle, almost as if he didn't want to hurt her by bringing this up. "William Dugan."

With all the calm she could muster, she set her water glass on a table before her hands could start to shake.

And, sure enough, they did.

Chapter Eleven

Christina's face went pale.

Derek had expected such a reaction. That's why he'd invited her over—so he could address what was worrying him without her being forced to put on an office game face for the rest of the day.

Last week, he'd contacted some business connections, slowly putting together details that weren't exactly listed on Christina's résumé. And he'd finally discovered why she'd been so skittish around him, why she'd decided their night together had been a "mistake."

God, he felt like a fool for the way he'd treated her. For the way he'd tried to make her admit that it had been so right, that it hadn't been wrong at all.

Setting down his own glass of water, Derek leaned

his forearms on his jeans-clad thighs. "Can you tell me your side of the story, Christina? I talked to several people, but I want to hear what you have to say."

She smoothed a hand over the crease of her shorts, avoided meeting his gaze. "You heard the basics, I'm sure. I cried harassment, Dugan cried denial and, in the end, I cried all the way to Los Angeles. Just so you know, I don't make a habit of suing my bosses. Are you worried about that?"

"Good question."

That got her attention. She whipped her gaze up to him, hurt.

"I suppose I can't blame you for feeling that way," she said.

"Wait. What I meant is that it's something a decent boss would consider, but I don't believe for a second that you'd ever do something so underhanded."

"Then…" She tilted her head. "You believe my side of the story?"

She looked so sweet, so open.

He wanted to take her in his arms, soothe her. But he could only sit there, mindful of how she'd no doubt feel about him touching her again.

"I believe you, Christina. Since you quit Macrizon, William Dugan has been sued by two more female co-workers."

Nodding, Christina exhaled. "I kept in touch with some of the employees. The cases are still pending, so we'll see if Dugan finally gets his due. Back when

I brought charges, no one took me seriously. He was too rich, too influential and my complaints were dismissed because of a lack of evidence. But if I hadn't done it, I wouldn't have been able to live with myself."

"Why didn't you tell me about this before?"

She paused, considering. "A lot of reasons. It isn't exactly something you advertise to your new boss. 'Hey, by the way, I accused a former employer of harassing me with constantly lewd comments, sexual situations and the threat of losing my job if I didn't put out. But you can trust me and feel good about working with me anyway.'"

"I see your point." Derek was trying not to sound bruised. "But I thought we had more than an office relationship."

"Derek…" She sighed. "You know that it was a good idea for us to stop before things got ugly. I'm sorry for putting us both in this position, but for once in my life, I couldn't help myself…."

She left the sentence hanging, a wisp of steam rising, then dissipating.

"I'm glad you lost control," he said.

Christina looked away, started to push back a stray hair from her forehead before stopping, probably realizing her hair was entirely in place.

As usual.

"I'm glad, too," she said, "even though it won't happen again."

His fantasies did a free fall at her words, but how

could he blame her? Her background put a wrench
into having a casual affair. Hell, he'd been lucky that
she'd let him in for even one night.

Still, he heard himself saying, "What if we could
keep our extracurricular activities under wraps?
Would that matter?"

There. That sounded more like the old Rockwell.
Stopping at nothing to get what he wanted. A man
who relied on that "animal magnetism" to seek out
a no-strings-attached good time.

It's not as if he were asking her to have some kind
of long-term affair. Not at all. When the San Antonio offices of Fortune-Rockwell became profitable
again, who knew how long he'd be around.

Don't stay in one place—or with one woman—
too long. That was his philosophy. Walk away while
everything was still good.

"To be honest," she said, "I'm sorely tempted.
God knows I am, but carrying on with my boss
would be like holding my hand over a flame to see
how long I could take the heat before I got burned."

Ouch. "I'm sure there's not that much pain involved."

He added a killer grin, just to be that much more
convincing.

"Stop, Derek." She laughed gently, no stranger to
his technique. "You can't win me over this time. Last
week's gossip was a close call, and I'd be stupid not
to pay attention to the warning. Loose talk is a
mighty corporate weapon."

Hell, he'd given it the old college try. But he wasn't done questioning her about that other matter. "I heard you were also scorched by some fellow employees during the harassment suit."

"Yes, Rebecca Waters. I have no proof, but I know she spread the word that *I* was the one who came on to Dugan."

"Why would she do that?"

Clearly miffed, Christina shrugged. "Long story. Let's just say Rebecca took great pleasure in bringing other women down for some psychologically tweaked reason. In the beginning, Gloria and I were friends with Rebecca. We did everything together at work, after work… But Rebecca did drugs, and she got my sister started down the wrong path. When I tried to talk some sense into Gloria, Rebecca took offense."

"So she weakened your case against Dugan out of revenge." Women could be so damned toxic.

"You got it. And last week, with Twyla's rumors, all this came back to haunt me. It was almost like I'd never left Macrizon."

Derek's sight went red. "Dammit, I wish *I'd* been Rebecca's boss. There'd have been hell to pay."

Immediately, he wanted to take the comment back. Not because Christina's eyes had widened in grateful wonder. He kind of liked that. But because getting this defensive about a woman wasn't in his playbook.

Clearing his throat, he tried to seem less emotional. Christina could definitely handle herself. She didn't need him around to fight battles for her. He didn't even need to be doing it, period.

She must have sensed his backtracking, because she continued, talking around his outburst, letting him off the hook.

"You know the worst part about Macrizon?" she asked. "Gloria didn't believe me. That's when I quit the firm and left my family. I was angry at the injustice of it all, the shame of accusing someone and coming out looking the fool. Facing them was impossible."

Touched by her vulnerability once again—it'd take a man of stone not to be—Derek rested a hand on her bare knee. It wasn't an overture, and she seemed to understand this, hesitating, reaching out to touch her fingertips to his.

"You could never be a failure," he said. "You're brilliant, Christina Mendoza. And the amount of courage it took to step up and seek justice from a powerful man who'd wronged you…" He turned his hand over, clasping her fingers. "Your bravery blows my mind."

For a moment, she didn't say anything, only watched him with a shine to her eyes.

"Coming from you, that means a lot," she said.

Now it was his turn to blush. Yeah, *blush*. Or maybe the late afternoon sun had gotten to him.

That had to be it. First, he'd chattered out too much information about his family life. Then there was that knight-to-the-rescue declaration. Now, this.

Could Christina mess up his existence any more? Derek was scaring the living soul out of himself with all these damned self-discoveries.

During the ensuing pause, they both held on to their water glasses, sipped at them, watched the river. The weakening sun flashed off the surface while canoes and boats coasted by.

"So how's the rowing coming?" she asked.

Derek almost fell off his chair in relief. Thank God for a change of subject. Not that he was sorry he'd brought up the whole Dugan conversation—it needed to be addressed—but...

He was sorry she'd ended up scrambling his brain so much.

"I'm still working out every morning," he said. "I've got a couple of months until the Water Safari."

"Sounds fun." A breeze picked up, fluttering her dark ponytail. "I've never rowed, canoed, kayaked...anything like that."

"Then I guess I'll have to take you sometime."

Bam! He'd said it before thinking. Water time was Derek time, a groove of peace he kept all to himself during the quiet of morning or dusk.

But, somehow, sharing his passion for the sport with Christina didn't seem all that out of line.

"I'd really love that," she said.

She smiled, blindsiding him.

Enchanted, he lowered his voice, revved up by her interest. "How about tonight, Christina? Late. After Richie goes home. A midnight row."

His body primed itself with heat, just at the thought of the possibilities. Moonlight, water…absolute seduction material.

But he shouldn't be thinking like that. What a letch.

She took so long to answer, Derek thought that maybe he hadn't asked at all.

Finally, she spoke. "If we go, it would be on a friendly basis. There can't be anything…you know. *Beyond.*"

Though his instinct was to pursue the matter, to convince her into saying yes, Derek restrained himself.

He knew why she was saying no, and he couldn't disrespect how she felt. But it'd been worth a try.

A knock on the sliding glass door captured his attention. Richie, standing there with his Opie-red hair and thick glasses.

Poor guy. If Derek ever had a child—unlikely as it was—he'd never relegate the kid to a spot on the calendar that appeared only once a month. He knew too well how it felt to be alienated by your dad, deserted by your mom.

Without hesitation, Derek got to his feet, opened the door and mussed Richie's hair, bringing a smile to the boy's face.

"I'm hungry," the kid said.

Derek checked his watch. Almost dinnertime, all right. Sandra, Richie's mom, had said she'd be back late tonight, and Derek had just planned on asking the boy what kind of pizza he wanted. Simple.

But he doubted the kid ate anything but fast food for a regular diet. Based on what Richie said, Sandra wasn't exactly what you'd call a cook.

"You want to go over to La Villita for some grub?" Derek asked Richie.

Grinning, Christina crossed one tanned leg over the other as she watched him deal with a miniperson. It was a much more subtle process than corporate wheeling-and-dealing, and she looked real entertained by that fact, bobbing her tennis shoe up and down.

Derek was so caught up in her that he almost didn't hear Richie's answer.

"La Villita." Richie seemed interested. "We studied that in school. It's San Antonio's first neighborhood."

"You told me," he said, tearing his gaze away from Christina. "I remember you said something about getting an A on your project for it. We can have steak or seafood… Whatever you want."

"I like hamburgers."

"All right, then." Hell, Derek was striking out all over the place. "Get your jacket. It's on the chair by the door."

After Derek let the child go, he noticed Christina's amused lift of the brow.

"What?" he asked.

"Score for you. You're good with him."

He hoped she wasn't thinking like other women: how baby-sitting would translate into a nursery in a suburban house with topiaries and swing sets.

But so what if she was? Christina didn't even want a short, hot fling with him.

Richie, clad in a green windbreaker, scooted right back, ducking his head out the door to address Christina. "You hungry, too?"

"I don't..."

Stubborn lady. Even so, Derek didn't want her to go home yet.

"Yeah," he said, goading her. "Why don't you come with us? A friendly outing, of course."

"Well... It's a chaperoned field trip?" she asked, a sparkle in her eyes.

"Safe as can be."

Christina put on a mock show of really turning this over in her mind, and that's when Derek knew she'd be coming with them.

Friend: 1. Fling: 0.

He'd just have to live with it.

For tonight, at least.

The south bank of the San Antonio River was home to La Villita, with its historically preserved buildings, which housed art studios, crafts stores, shops and restaurants. Originally, Spanish soldiers from the Alamo—or what was then known as Mission San Antonio Valero—had settled here in primitive huts until a flood washed the structures away.

Nature's wrath had then made way for German and French immigrants, then a decline into a slum until the city fathers decided to preserve the village.

Christina had learned all this and more during dinner with Richie and Derek at the Guadalajara Grill. Over Tex-Mex and Richie's favorite meal—a burger—they'd laughed together, talked about Richie's school, compared different video games and how they rated.

Afterward, they killed time by strolling the cobblestoned streets past shops constructed of caliche block and limestone. In five minutes, they were scheduled to meet Richie's mom so she could introduce her son to her date—who seemed to be the next Mr. Right, after all—then take the child home.

Full of energy at the prospect of seeing "Mommy," Richie had darted ahead, putting on the brakes only to inspect the display window of a mercantile.

Alone at last, thought Christina. Oh, no.

"I didn't realize you were into video games," Derek said, a teasing glint in his gaze.

"What can I say? *Grand Theft Auto* keeps me coming back for more." She didn't mention that, in her entertainment center next to her yoga DVDs, she had a small collection of those stress-relieving games.

Junk food for the mind.

They were walking side by side, the light hairs on his arm brushing her skin every few seconds. Even though she could've moved away, putting some much-needed space between them, she didn't.

Not after their talk today. As she'd unburdened

herself about William Dugan, Christina had felt a great weight lift from her body, something permanent she'd been trying to achieve for years with running and exercise.

But Derek's understanding had made it so much easier to breathe now.

As they approached the mercantile, he casually guided her with his fingertips on the small of her back.

The contact was innocent. Nice. Fit for an old-fashioned starlit walk.

So why had his touch sent a naughty, very modern zing up her spine?

Richie didn't look at them, just kept staring at the bath products displayed in the window.

"Think he'll be okay?" the child asked.

He was talking about his mom's date. Christina felt so badly for Richie. At dinner, he'd talked about "Mommy" as if she'd hung the moon but, from what Derek had said earlier, it sounded as if the woman had taken up residence there most of the time, too. Without Richie.

"If he's not okay," Derek said, resting a hand on Richie's small shoulder, "you tell me."

There it was again, that protective side of him, overwhelming her with a dizzy warmth.

So dependable. Trustworthy.

"Really?" Richie asked. "You'd beat him up for me?"

"Well, not beat—"

Richie had turned around, fixing a look of such heartbreaking adoration on his baby-sitter that it made Christina cover her chest with an opened hand.

Derek shrugged. "I'd do my best to help you out, Richie. Definitely."

A huge grin split the boy's face, and Derek stuck his hands on his hips, concentrating on the mercantile window, the ghost of a smile on his own mouth.

What had happened to Patrick's "predatory pride and joy"?

Was this actually the same business shark?

Christina's heart thumped loudly under her palm, tapping out a message: *Fall-ing. Fall-ing.*

A female voice shouted out Richie's name from down the street, near a plaza. They all turned to find his mom, decked out in date finery, with her arms opened for her son.

With a jump of joy, Richie launched himself at Derek, clamping his arms around his waist. "Thank you for the food. This was lots of fun."

"I had a great time, too." Gingerly, Derek patted the boy's back. "Don't be a stranger, okay?"

"I won't." Richie disengaged and was immediately on Christina, hugging her, also. She bent down, returning the affection.

Wishing that someday she could…

She cut off the surprisingly domestic thought as Richie backed away.

"You think you'll come over so we can play?" he asked. "You'd be a real good Jedi."

"I could manage a visit." She smiled. "Maybe I'll see you around."

As Richie said one last, "Cool," then took off, Christina stood again. Both she and Derek watched the boy dash toward his mom, who scooped him into her arms and waved. A man, decent-looking and somewhat hesitant, waited in the wings.

The date.

"He looks nice," Christina said, waving back.

"Bet he's another loser. If he is, I'm going to have a talk with Sandra. It's hard enough to keep my mouth shut about her ex-husband, but if she asks my opinion—"

"How can you have an opinion?" Gently, she tugged on his shirt. "You haven't met this guy."

When he captured her searching gaze with his own, his eyes had darkened to black. "I haven't met him *yet*."

Oh, this man, she thought. He'd defended Christina just as tenaciously in the face of adversity, too. But how long would it last with *her*? Was he offering the boy something he couldn't offer to women?

Curious, she touched his elbow. In response, he shot her a halfhearted grin, then took her arm and led her toward the welcoming light of an open antique shop.

Was it a good idea to remind him that their chaperone was gone and it was time to call it a night?

She nestled her fingers further into the crook of his muscular arm.

Nah. She was at ease with him, with no expectations, their rules laid out in front of them like a brick-solid road.

There'd be no seductive surprises tonight, just a harmless stroll around La Villita, right?

Even if the moon was out, bathing him in shadow and light, making the night—and him—more mysterious.

When he walked her into the safety of the store, she relaxed. The shopkeeper acknowledged them, then went back to reading her *Entertainment Weekly* magazine.

The scent of musty wood and dried flowers mixed into a heady brew as she sauntered to the back of the place while inspecting the merchandise: rusted lanterns, stained glass windows, pictographs and faded clothing.

One item in particular caught her attention—a red shawl, worked with an intricate pattern of roses.

Won over, Christina touched it, felt the silky lace glide over her fingers. Normally, she didn't wear bold colors. They brought too much attention to a person who usually sought to avoid it.

But what if she were the kind of woman who felt confident in clothing such as this? A Spanish señorita at a fiesta, flirting with the *caballeros*. A lady of quality on her balcony, fixing a rose into her dark hair as her man watched from the shadows.

The romance got to her, made her wonder how the sight of her in something so lovely and free would effect Derek.

She felt him move up behind her, ease the shawl off its hanger.

"You like this," he said. "I could tell, even from across the store."

He was so close that she could feel the vibration of his voice through the skin of her back. She shivered, wanting him to say more.

Instead, he slipped the shawl over her shoulders, then unbound her hair.

It felt like she'd been submerged in a pool of petals, bathed in smooth, luxurious silk.

When his hands rested on her shoulders, stroking the material over her, Christina's knees melted to oil.

"Let me buy it for you," he whispered.

If they were just two people who didn't have a care in the world, she could imagine going home with him, stripping off her boring clothes and emerging only with the shawl wrapped around her body. Her skin would peek through the lace, taunting him as he watched her from the bed, desiring her.

Making her feel as alive as he had only days ago.

But they weren't those people. They had their places in the world, and neither of them cared to step away from their jobs long enough to surrender their identities.

With reluctance, she removed the shawl, then replaced it on the hanger. Even without looking at Derek, she knew he was disappointed.

Yet so was she.

"I'm not the type to wear red." She smiled up at him to ease the tension that suddenly permeated the room.

His intense, dark gaze reflected his need, echoing that night at the riverside salsa bar. He was ready to pounce, famished for her.

Would it be like this all the time now? They hadn't gotten each other out of their systems at all, had they? Their need had only boiled over. Become more dangerous.

Trying to keep matters in hand, Christina walked away from Derek, stretching that good-idea distance between them. When she spotted some candy, she decided to busy herself with lusting after that instead of her boss.

He left her alone at the back of the store, but that was fine by her. She'd require a cooling-off period before facing him again anyway.

A few minutes later, she was ready, a paper sack of lemon drops in hand. After purchasing it, she found him outside, waiting for her.

Grinning, he jerked his chin toward the candy.

"Couldn't resist, could you?"

Er...the candy? Or him?

Opening the bag, she offered him first choice. With a, "Why not?" he took one.

"Sometimes I just can't help myself," she said as they walked in the direction of the parking lot. It was as if both of them knew that separating for the night was the best course of action.

"Any more secrets I should know about you?" he asked. "Besides all the fattening food and the scariness of that hidden video game fetish?"

Not to mention William Dugan. She was happy he didn't say it out loud.

"Nope. Today was the last of the secrets."

But what about you? she felt like asking. *Tell me what you're hiding. Because I've seen it in your eyes so many times. The bitterness. The isolation.*

Asking him would've been opening a Pandora's box, and Christina knew better. She might as well leave things as they were now, with an easy companionship just hovering over their attraction. Digging deeper would get her in over her head.

Or would it make her fall just a little more?

They'd driven their own vehicles to La Villita so, as they said their goodbyes in the public parking lot, there was a Saturday night crowd swarming around them. Keeping her in check. Taking away the spell of being alone with him.

Still, as they parted ways, she couldn't help looking back over her shoulder. Just one last peek.

He was watching her, too, thumbs hooked in the pockets of his jeans.

Their shared glance jolted her, made her want to run back to him, cover him in shawl-soft kisses.

But, instead, as mist from the river filtered through the light from a street lamp, then down to him, he raised his hand.

Bye.

She did the same, almost feeling as if she were using her palm to push him away.

That night, her sleep was restless, brimming with sweet, impossible dreams of him. Dreams painted with sighs, red lace, diamonds sparkling with the fervor of Gloria's engagement ring.

And when she woke up the next morning, she found a package on her doorstep. Brown paper wrapped around a gift.

The shawl.

As she stood on her threshold in her robe, holding the present to her face, taking in the scent of roses and old memories, Christina felt her heart stumble.

A prelude to the ultimate fall.

Chapter Twelve

Sunday morning, Derek missed Christina's phone call because he was out on the river.

But the sound of her voice on the answering machine shook him up all the same.

I got your gift, she'd said. *Thank you, Derek. You seem to know how to make me happy.*

Of course, he'd glowed for the rest of the day, smiling to himself every once in a while as he caught up on office work in his condo.

How did she have such power over him? Either he couldn't figure it out or he didn't want to.

All Derek knew was that the sight of her in the red shawl had not only aroused him physically, but emotionally, too.

When's the last time he'd impulsively wrapped a woman in his embrace like that? Never, that's when. He'd never wanted to hold on to someone so tightly, bundle them up to keep them warm and safe.

Even though she'd refused the shawl in the end, he'd known that she longed for it. So while she'd poked around the candy section, he'd purchased the item, coming back for it after they'd said goodbye in the parking lot.

Then delivering it to her door in the wee hours of the morning.

It'd taken a lot of strength not to knock, to beg to come in. But he'd done it, knowing Christina Mendoza was a woman who required respectful treatment.

When Monday morning rolled around, Derek was still consumed with her, but surely this stronger-than-usual infatuation would wear off soon.

Wouldn't it?

True to form, he arrived before the rest of the building did. Sometimes he even beat Christina to the office, but not today.

She was waiting in the chair by his desk, going over some reports, when he walked in. Surprisingly, she had her hair down, the dark-brown strands raining over her shoulders and tucked behind her ears. She was also wearing khaki slacks and a striking red blouse that brought out the glow of her skin, the shine of her eyes.

They'd been instructed to dress casually today, since a "team building leader" would be putting them through physical exercises later in the conference room. Derek was even planning to don some jeans himself.

After his heart stopped jumping up and down in gleeful excitement at the sight of her, it occurred to him that he wouldn't mind seeing her first thing in the morning all the time.

But he'd get over this.

Even if…

My God, she was so beautiful.

She was flashing a smile at him as he lay his brief-case on a table. "Hi. I was hoping to catch you before everyone else came trooping in."

He found that he couldn't look at her without losing a part of himself. But he forced himself to, keeping the desk between them as insurance.

"I'm all yours," he said, cringing at his words. They were too true.

Standing, she set her papers on the chair. "A phone call didn't seem to be sufficient for what you gave me."

"The shawl?" He shrugged, trying to convince himself that he hadn't been sending her more than just a gift. That the shawl hadn't actually been some kind of message.

But what the hell had he been trying to say?

"I…" She wandered closer. "I've never received anything so wonderful before. I want you to know that."

When he glanced up at her, he expected to find The Christina Blush veiling her face, the shyness and distance.

That wasn't what he got.

Instead, she was watching him intently, boldly. Deep emotion stirred in her gaze, drawing him in, inviting him to claim it.

Her expression took the air right out of him, making time stop. He was sorely aware of her, of the images spinning in his mind.

Sir telling little Derek that he needed discipline, commitment to win in life, then forcing his son to hold up his shaking hands for two full hours just to prove his point.

Sir commanding his son to stand guard over Mom's open casket at the funeral, never allowing him to leave his post, even when Derek couldn't bear to see her unmoving body another second.

In a change of pattern, Derek then saw himself joining the Marines, ignoring Sir's phone calls and letters.

Sir's own funeral, attended by only five people, where Derek hesitated when he accepted the folded flag that had covered his father's coffin.

Derek dating woman after woman, overcompensating, bucking any kind of structure, just to prove his point to the world.

Rattled, Derek glanced away, wanting to chase off the memories as well as Christina's silent offer of something more than he could return.

"You looked good in the shawl," he said, forcing a grin, the gesture weighing heavily. "So I bought it."

She just stood there, tracing the edge of his desk with her finger. "Oh. All right."

Had she interpreted the shawl to mean something more?

Well, it had. But admitting it would take Derek in a direction he wasn't willing to travel.

The truth was that he'd merely been swept away by his libido during the weekend. Shaping this gift into some kind of grand gesture would be a mistake.

"Ready for our meeting?" he asked, desperate to concentrate on work—his savior.

"Sure." She smoothed down her slacks and backed away, retrieving her papers. "See you in the conference room in an hour then?"

"Will do." Derek concerned himself with booting up his computer.

As she left his office, his regret grew, blinding him to his surroundings.

Forget Fortune-Rockwell.

Why had he been such a jerk to her? Why had he turned her away, just as she'd been opening up to him?

Swiveling his chair so he faced his grand window view of San Antonio, Derek berated himself for pushing her away.

It was a lecture far worse than any of Sir's had been.

Christina placed information packets before every conference room chair, preparing for the meeting. Seth had developed the bright idea of hosting a management retreat, just to strengthen the impression that Fortune-Rockwell was starting anew, that they all needed to bond in order to make this branch successful again.

Today, they were interviewing a team building leader who specialized in encouraging employees to be more positive, to trust their co-workers through exercises. Therapy.

Lord knew Christina needed some herself.

What had she been doing, laying herself on the line with Derek like that? Oh, boy, had it been a mistake.

To think, she'd been willing to express her growing feelings for him. To tell him she was ready to take things to the next level, whatever that meant. She'd never gotten past square two of a relationship, so this was all new to her. Exciting.

Hope defying.

She'd tried to articulate to him how much that shawl meant. The gift had shown her that he'd looked deep inside her soul and noticed her burning need to be desired and loved. No man had ever paid such attention to her, looking beyond the prim suits and cool attitude.

But Derek was different, she'd thought. He could see through her, into her.

Christina should've known better. When God had been giving out luck with men, she'd gotten to the front of the line only to have them run plum out of it.

Heck, she was used to burying herself in work to avoid this pain, and she'd just go right back to doing it. *No problemo.*

She'd recover. Someday.

Even though she'd already lost her heart to the guy.

Yes, she was hopelessly enamored. During the course of their working relationship, her itty-bitty crush had turned into something much scarier.

And more sublime.

Over the next few minutes, the casually dressed personal development team—Seth, Jonathan, Adam and Ben—reported to the conference room, and she was there to meet them with a pasted-on smile. Good old responsible Christina, the woman dedicated to her professional calling. Yes, that was her. Still.

Soon, the team building leader arrived, as did Jack and Derek, who sat in the seat next to her, dressed in jeans, a button-down and his work boots. His clothes reminded her of their weekend, the casual ruffle of his hair, the family man demeanor.

As everyone settled down for the meeting, Christina accidentally glanced at him, discovering that he was already watching her, an apology in his gaze.

Blood kicking in her veins, she didn't know how to respond. Had something changed since this morning?

When his hand skimmed over her thigh under the table, Christina thought she could maybe take a good guess.

The meeting started, and she took his hand in hers, holding her breath to see how he'd react.

He ran his thumb over her fingers, stroking, setting her at ease.

Oh, but she was melting again. Not good. Businesswomen didn't turn to slush in the middle of important meetings.

They managed to hide their contact for a while, linking pinkies, playing a bout of squeeze tag, basically attempting to seem very serious above the table.

Then the team building leader asked them to get to their feet for a sample of one of his "trust exercises."

It was the one where someone stands on the table, falls backward without looking and everyone catches the victim.

"I hate this kind of stuff," Derek whispered in Christina's ear as they lined up on opposite sides to face each other. The scent of her hair wove around his thoughts.

"Focus on work," she whispered back.

He couldn't wait for a break so he could talk to her, tell her…what? That he wanted to sleep with her again and that's it?

Jonathan, a really tiny guy, had volunteered to take the initial fall, so he climbed on the table, telling the participants that they'd better catch him or else.

Derek took the opportunity to send Christina a smile—not one of his gimme-some grins, either. This one was filled with a softness he hadn't known he'd possessed.

Across the aisle, Jack saw it, brow cocking in question.

In fact, after all of them had taken their turns falling—frightening as hell, that exercise—they took a break, and Jack intercepted Derek before he could take Christina aside.

His partner took him into Derek's nearby office, then shut the door. "What was *that?*"

"I know." Derek played dumb. "Damned head-shrinking exercises."

"No, that's not what I'm talking about." Jack's blue eyes were saucered with surprise, and not even in a bad way. "I saw those puppy-love looks you were giving Christina."

"Aw, come on. Just because you got engaged doesn't mean the rest of the world is riding on hearts, Jack."

"You're so full of…" His partner shook a finger at him. "I've been noticing a definite metamorphosis. Back in New York, I knew a man who was aggressive and one immovable warrior. But something happened here. Ever since Christina Mendoza walked into your office…"

Panic needled Derek. "I haven't lost my edge."

"Not in business. But you haven't been seen around town with a string of women, either. What happened?"

"I'll be getting into the swing of the San Antonio social life. I just need the time to do it. Don't worry."

"And your hair?"

Derek touched it. "What?"

"It's longer." Jack gestured to his own black strands. "My mom was the one who mentioned it, because women don't let any detail go unnoticed."

"Oh." So Derek hadn't gone for his weekly cut. Big deal. Ever since Christina had mentioned the military-like precision of his style, it'd bothered Derek. Growing it out felt damned good.

"I'm worried for you." Jack plopped onto the leather couch. "Too many weird changes."

Could this be true? Jack, Derek's own self-appointed nemesis, was concerned?

A smile burst over his face. He'd finally hit that home run over the far fence, and Jack was here to see it.

His big-brother figure continued, shaking his head. "I thought you'd be the last man standing, Derek, impervious to love."

Love? LOVE? Who said anything about…?

Had he gone and done it with Christina? And was it that damned obvious?

Stunned, Derek started pacing, trying to find a way out of this box he found himself in. "Christina deserves a guy who can commit."

"Absolutely."

"And that's never been my style."

Jack paused, giving Derek time to realize how stupid he sounded.

"Why not?" asked his partner.

Yeah, why not?

Because, even now, when he'd halfway admitted his feelings for her, he was short of breath, scared witless.

But, even without having Jack lecture him about

the joys of falling for a woman—which he started to do anyway, just because he claimed more experience—Derek knew he could never settle down enough to make Christina happy.

Being a numbers guy, he knew the bottom line.

And this was it.

When Derek had taken off with Jack during the break, Christina had been left to wonder what the heck was going on.

Wasn't there a lot to say to each other?

Of course, they were at work, which made that sort of talk all the riskier. Maybe, at the end of the day, they could safely hash things out?

On her way back to her own office—she just had to check her e-mail—Twyla found her, asking if they could talk.

Once there, they sat in opposing chairs, Christina facing the petite blonde who'd tried to bring her down with words.

"How can I help you, Twyla?" Not as rude as she wanted to be, but not entirely welcoming, either.

"I wanted to touch base, if that's okay." Her subordinate handed over a stack of bound papers. "Everything you need to know about Fortune-Rockwell's new personal development classes and more."

The young worker beamed at a job well done and, as Christina leafed through the documents, she couldn't help but to be impressed.

"This is excellent," she said. "Thank you, Twyla."

"You're welcome." She didn't make a move to leave.

"Anything else?"

"Yes." She took a deep breath, exhaled. "I was wondering if I could be allowed back on your team."

If Twyla hadn't broached the subject, Christina would have. She'd thought a lot about giving Twyla a second chance, but something unexpected had happened since she'd returned to Red Rock.

Christina had gained confidence.

And she'd come to realize that allowing an employee to backstab her yet again was a slap in the face, not only to her, but to the team members who'd worked their rear ends off to keep their ethics intact.

Avoiding the trap of seeming superior, Christina carefully worded her response. "What you did, Twyla, didn't make a very good case for your return. You showed disrespect for me, and that can never be erased."

Visions of Rebecca Waters and her vengeful attitude kept Christina strong in her convictions.

She continued, even as her assistant's posture crumbled.

"I'm sure you can understand why I think we should part ways, Twyla. You can have a fresh start in another department."

"But Derek's team is the prestigious one."

So she'd been playing the flirting card to move up the corporate food chain, Christina thought. Tempting the men on the team with her smile and provocative comments. Flashing cleavage to Derek. Using gossip to oust the competition.

Christina stood from her chair, tacitly dismissing Twyla. "You'll do solid work elsewhere in the company. I've no doubt about that. Good luck."

Gripping the arms of her chair until her knuckles were white, Twyla didn't move. She merely kept a bead on Christina.

"You're not such hot stuff just because you got cozy with the boss," she said. "Anyone can do that, you know."

Even though Christina knew Derek hadn't been sampling from the office, the words still tore at her.

Or was she wrong? Was Derek so good at keeping his affairs undercover that she just didn't know about them?

"Twyla," Christina opened her door, waiting for the girl to leave, "you might want to stop now, before you do even more damage to your career."

"I've got Jack Fortune in my cheering section." Twyla made herself at home, crossing her arms over her chest while leaning back into the cushions. "I'm not going anywhere."

We'll see about that, Christina thought.

"Derek's going to make sure of it, too," Twyla added.

Unable to move, to even function, Christina merely stood in place, holding on to the door for support.

"You're too stubborn to ask," Twyla said, "so I'll spell it out."

"I don't want to hear your vitriol—"

"This is how Derek works." Twyla finally stood, coming face-to-face with Christina. The smaller woman's spiky pumps gave her some height, some power. "Everyone knows he eats women for breakfast. Think about it, Christina. Why not take advantage of that weakness?"

It was like seeing a car lose control and screech off a highway, slowly flying through the air, then crashing into a building. Christina couldn't stop watching, listening, waiting for the explosion.

"Business is not a battleground, Twyla." Right. Hadn't she spent years disproving that theory?

Her employee was staring at her, knowing Christina was grasping at straws, trying to stay afloat in her own world of self-delusion.

She couldn't admit that Derek was one of *them*. As much of an enemy as William Dugan.

"Now, I haven't been with Derek myself," Twyla said. "At least, not yet. But it's only a matter of time. Playboys get around."

Crash! There it was. All the doubts Christina had harbored about him. All the disappointment she'd forced on herself because she'd brought sex into the office when she knew better.

"Get out." Christina stood at her door, her face a study in cool composure.

But judging by the grin on Twyla's mouth, she'd done her job.

"I'll get back on the team," she said as she

walked past, "with or without your help. I'll do it *my* way."

Christina wanted to tell the girl that females like Twyla gave businesswomen a bad name.

And Derek a bad reputation.

Still, her suspicions returned full force. *Playboy. Womanizer.*

Just because he'd held her hand this morning, did that mean he wouldn't drop her like a hot stone by the end of the week?

She'd done it again, hadn't she? Let down her defenses and made yet another work situation impossible to handle.

When would she learn?

Shutting her door, Christina leaned against it, suddenly exhausted. But after a moment, she straightened up, realizing something.

She *had* learned.

Gradually, she'd realized that this bitterness about Dugan was holding her back. That she needed to let go of it in order to move on. And move on she would.

Should she go to a place where no one knew her before the situation became unbearable? Leave Fortune-Rockwell, which seemed to get uglier by the week, to start over?

But, dammit, she'd run away before, and it'd just brought her back to square one.

Yet it didn't have to be that way, not anymore. If Christina could clear her slate now, she could make her life better, never repeating the past again.

It was the best solution.

Resolute, Christina returned to the conference room, where the team building leader was ready to begin another bonding exercise: a simple pyramid.

She took care to stay away from Derek, although she could feel the heat of his gaze upon her, asking her to glance back at him.

To connect, just as they had this weekend.

But she wouldn't. She'd stay self-contained and safe.

"As in business," said the leader, a peppy little man in a company polo shirt, "we need a strong foundation on the bottom. Who would you all choose as your floor level?"

"Don't mind if I sit this one out," Jack said, ambling over to a chair, where he grinned and watched the action.

While the guys on the team chose Derek, Seth and Ben to be the foundation, Jack winked at Christina.

Dios. Why a wink?

The team shuffled, getting ready for the building process, but Derek took a detour, brushing past Christina.

"Can we talk?" he asked.

"What about?"

"Christina, look at me, dammit."

She couldn't. Just couldn't. She'd lose her common sense, her determination to move on if she... did.

He was watching her with such tenderness that

Christina almost nestled against his chest, seeking reassurance.

Fighting the temptation, she finally won, knowing that she couldn't stay on this hamster wheel, running in place forever.

Besides, it didn't matter if Derek Rockwell couldn't love her back. She'd spent her whole life knowing love was for other people. That all she'd have was man temptation and that's it.

"Mr. Rockwell?" said the leader.

With a gentle smile, Derek asked Christina, "Later?"

She didn't answer, just tried to focus as Jonathan and Adam were chosen for the pyramid's second level. She'd be the pinnacle.

As the two guys took their places, a prone Derek took the brunt of their weight, since he was in the center of the base.

"Aren't you going to tell them to get off your back, Derek?" Jack asked. "I hear it every day from you."

Her boss laughed, music to Christina's ears. In a perfect world, she could hear that sound for the rest of her life and never get tired of it.

But, suddenly, seeing him having a good time saddened her. How could she just stand here, pretending everything was okay?

Making believe that they were nothing more than boss and employee and that there was nothing going on between them was killing her.

"Christina?" asked the leader, inviting her to join them.

Simmering with pent-up emotions, she struggled to get to the top, wobbling, balancing so she wouldn't fall.

Even though she already had. For Derek. And hard.

She was sick of keeping everything back, of hiding what she felt, of running behind her books when the going got tough.

Remaining silent gave your power to other people, she thought. She couldn't do that anymore.

No more. Twyla's words weren't going to ruin her. And neither were office secrets.

No more bitterness.

"Derek?" she said.

"Yeah." He was so strong that she didn't hear any strain in his voice.

"I need a word with you."

"Now?"

"Now."

"Wait." The team builder stood in front of them, hands pushed out. "See how long you can hold each other up."

"I'm so tired of all these games," she said.

The team builder looked crushed.

"No, not yours," Christina said, swaying and recovering with the force of what she needed to do. "Office hide-and-seek. Gossip. Never being able to be a real person because you're too afraid of saying the wrong thing and being reprimanded for it. Cowering from people with more influence."

"Christina?"

It was both a warning and a question from Derek, but she was beyond holding anything back.

"We give people the power to undermine us," she added, too far gone to stop now. Speaking out felt *good*. "And I'm taking that power back."

Jonathan tried to glance up at her, but he faltered, making the entire pyramid tilt.

"Derek," she said, "I've gone and fallen in love with you."

Someone—her boss?—cursed, and their structure wavered. Then, with a burst of grunts and yells, they all came tumbling down.

For a second, they all sat on the carpet, gaping at each other.

Derek, himself, looked as if he'd been KO'd by the world heavyweight champion.

He didn't have to say anything for Christina to know she'd overstepped her bounds.

"I'm sorry," she said, rising to her feet, already on her way to the door. "But it's out, and I feel better than I have in years."

"Christina…" Derek's voice was choked.

She passed Jack, wanting so badly to leave, to escape Derek's oncoming rejection while she had the chance.

"I'll fax my resignation letter by the end of the day," she said.

And, with that, she shut the conference room door, knowing from experience that, just because you'd spoken out, it didn't mean you were going to be the better for it.

But, this time, unlike with William Dugan, she knew she would be.

Chapter Thirteen

She was in love with him?

Her declaration sent his world flip-flopping. Turning right side up, where it should've been in the first place.

Suddenly, everything—his refusal to settle down, his constant running from commitment—whirled away, leaving images in its wake.

Sitting at home on Saturday nights, eating popcorn and watching movies with Christina.

Spiriting her away to a quiet countryside cottage, where he could have her all to himself with no interference.

Laughing at the dinner table with their child,

just as easily as they had with his little neighbor, Richie.

Uh-huh, Derek Rockwell had been taken down.

Even though the other team members, plus Jack, were all ogling him like guppies gasping for oxygen, Derek couldn't get to his feet.

He doubted his legs would hold him up even if he tried.

"You're just sitting here after what she said?" Seth asked, rubbing his knees from the crash.

"Man," added Adam, "that's cold."

Cold. Stone damned cold. Just like Sir.

But, as Derek had been trying to tell himself for all of his life, he wasn't his father.

Well, it was damned time to really prove it.

He struggled to a stand, stomach silly with butterflies.

Winged creatures tickling his gut. This was new to him, but he kind of liked it.

Actually, he liked it a lot.

Jack had come to stand in front of him, looking so smug that Derek wanted to rearrange his face.

"You going to take care of this?" Jack asked, voice rushed and anxious. "Not only is she a hell of an analyst, Derek, she's a hell of a woman. Talk her out of quitting. And while you're at it—"

"I know exactly what I'm going to do."

All the guys who'd fallen when Derek's arms had given out at the "I love you" declaration yelled at him.

"Get out of here, man."

"Go get her!"

"As I was saying," Derek said, backing toward the door, "I'm on my way."

Jack thumped him on the back, and off he went. Even though some joker said, "Does this mean a long lunch?" as he left, Derek let it go.

For now.

Christina couldn't quit. He wouldn't be able to stand a day without seeing her, without being privy to her intelligence and kindhearted smiles. Wouldn't be able to live with himself if he didn't take this risk.

Sure, she was a crackerjack analyst, but that was secondary to the woman inside.

He jogged down the halls, dodging employees, trying to catch the woman he loved—good God, *loved*—before she left the building.

Stopping by her office on the way to the elevators, he took the chance on seeing that she was there.

Bingo.

With haste, she was dumping personal items into a box, her back to the lobby windows.

As Derek caught his breath, his heart exploded in his chest, a crescendo of emotion to the dance they'd been performing together.

The dance of a strange but ultimately wonderful courtship.

She must have heard him quietly walk up behind her, because she froze, her hair curtaining the side of her face.

Derek reached out, pushed the strands back.

Still, she didn't look at him. "I'm making this easy on you since it'll be impossible to work with each other now."

"It will?"

She glanced at him, questions in her hazel eyes. "I put it *all* out there, Derek. And I meant what I said. I lost my professional judgment and fell in love with my boss. But I wouldn't take back what I said. Not if you paid me. I don't care who knows about how I feel for you. I don't care what they think."

"Good, because I think the word's bound to spread like wildfire." He stroked her hair again, changing her look to one of hopeful confusion. "Wait until someone calls Patrick to tell him the news. He'll be overjoyed."

"What news?" she said cautiously. "That I fired myself in a spectacular blaze of glory?"

"No." Cupping her face in both of his hands, Derek stroked his thumbs over the hollows of her cheekbones. "That I'm far gone for you, too."

She stared at him as if trying to decipher what he'd said. He remembered her sad ex-boyfriend stories, how her past had built a glass wall of low self-esteem around her year after year. So he hurried to reassure her.

Not that he was very good at it.

"The thing is," he said, "I'm having trouble getting the right phrase out. You know I've never said it before. But it's there, believe me."

So why was it so hard to say *I love you, Christina*?

Time to try again. "All my life, I've been making my best effort to be the opposite of my father. I overcompensated by dating Lite women, ones who didn't expect me to commit to them. Then you came along."

Her lips were parted, her brows knitted, as if she were wondering what exactly he was doing in her office, chattering away in the aftermath of her emotional doomsday in the conference room.

"What's a Lite woman?" she asked.

"The anti-you." He traced her jawline with his thumb. "Someone who cared as little as I did. See, my father—he made me call him Sir since he was a sergeant in the Army—well, he taught me that rules and regulations were the only way to survive in life. When I rebelled, he punished me, and that just made me more ornery. I decided I'd never walk in his polished-shoe steps, then started on what I believed was a different path."

Tentatively, Christina folded her hands around his, drawing them away from her face, pressing them near her collarbone, where she could rest her chin on them. She glanced up at him from beneath lowered eyelashes, stealing his heart yet again. Encouraging him to continue.

"When he was home, I had to make my bed for Sir. He'd try to bounce a quarter off of it. Usually, I failed to meet his standards, so I'd start the day with five hundred push-ups. And it just went from there."

"I could tell there was something going on with

you," she said. "The loneliness in your eyes when you'd talk about family. The way you didn't want to acknowledge them at all."

No one else, besides Patrick, had ever bothered to read between Derek's perfect lines. It was a miracle that he'd found someone who could.

"Odd," she added. "You tried to be so different from your dad, but on the outside, you aren't, really. The authoritative boss. The conservative demeanor."

She flicked his button-down shirt's opened collar. When he pulled the material away from his neck, he realized that it'd curled upward yet again.

"But then," she said, "there was always a part of you that wanted to be set free, I think."

"You're one of the only people who seems to understand that I was a slave to Sir's memory."

She smiled, no doubt still waiting for *that phrase*. The one that meant commitment, the one that had always been so hard for him to say.

But for this woman, he'd lay his soul on the line.

"Translated from Ultimate Bachelorspeak, all my blithering means I love you, Christina."

Whoosh...

It felt as if the world had fallen off his shoulders, stripping a facade away from him, revealing the heart he'd forgotten he had.

She'd closed her eyes, kissing one of his wrists. When she opened her gaze again, tears glimmered, spilling down her face.

"Did I say it wrong?" he asked.

"No. I like your translation just fine."

He became aware of employees lingering outside her office window, but he couldn't have cared less.

"There's Twyla," she said, her voice stronger as she glanced out the window, too. Even though she'd overcome the need to hide what was between her and Derek, she didn't want his own reputation to suffer for it.

But when she tried to pull away from him, restoring a professional distance, he wouldn't let her go.

Ecstatic, she settled right back into his arms.

Her ex-team member, who was in the midst of a gathering group in the lobby, glanced away, attempting to seem busy by scribbling on a notepad, nodding to her cohorts as if deep in the thrall of business.

The sight of Twyla only made Christina realize that her bitterness about the past was really gone. Kaput.

Once Derek had chased her down and confessed his own love, Christina's slate had been wiped clean, ready for new memories. Like the man she loved, she, too, could let go of her old hurts, making room in her heart for a much brighter future.

"Twyla?" Derek asked. "What about her?"

When she glanced back at him, he was grinning, teasing.

"Maybe your next business analyst will tell you all about Twyla and how she needs to be fired," she said, pushing at his chest as he laughed.

His mirth trailed away, and he tightened his grip

around her. "There won't be a next analyst. I'm going to talk the one we have into staying. She's much too valuable to let go. In a lot of ways."

She couldn't believe he was returning her affection.

She'd fantasized about this moment for so long that the real thing almost seemed like a dream, too.

"As much as I appreciate your compliments, Derek, we can't carry on as we were. Team dynamics would be uncomfortable. People would start to gossip again and that would be a distraction—it'd take away from employee efficiency."

He shook his head. "Carrying on? As I said, now that I have you, I'm not letting you go anywhere, Christina." He took a deep breath, then exhaled. "I'm going to marry you."

Fireworks exploded inside her chest, a celebration, a grand surprise she'd always hoped for, but never expected.

She wanted to hear it again, so she pretended she hadn't understood in the first place. "You...what?"

Bringing her hands to rest over his heart, he repeated himself.

"Marry me, Christina."

Instinctively, all her inner watchdogs rushed in to shield her, to make excuses: She and Derek hadn't known each other that long. This was still too new. What if, what if, what if...?

But, even if she'd told herself in the past that she'd never find love, an undying spark in her soul had always saved hope. It was this part of her that knew Derek was the one. Crazy as it seemed, a person didn't have to date for three months or even be engaged for one year to develop something beautiful.

Sometimes, she thought, rekindled, love flashed as quickly as lightning that needed to be captured. You just had to be brave enough to hold it to you, pain and all. To allow it to light up your soul with its eternal illumination.

"Even though you've always respected me," she said, "you also knew how to make me feel like a woman."

"Is that a yes?"

Though the question sounded doubtful, she could tell by the affection in his brown eyes that he knew what her answer would be.

"Yes, Derek. Yes!"

With a joyful laugh, he picked her up, twirled her in his arms. In return, she hugged him tightly.

Capturing her lightning.

When he finally set her down, he said, "Thank God. I don't think I could be happy without you, Christina. I believe I knew that the second you stepped into my office. It was just hell to admit."

"You were too busy ordering me around to notice."

As they laughed together, they realized there was quite a big audience outside the window. The employees weren't even bothering to hide their curiosity, watching them as if they were in a fishbowl, there to entertain.

Even the team, including Jack, was present. He was doing his best to peer at the contents of a folder while spying on them as he crossed the lobby.

"They're dying to know what's happening," she said.

Derek got a wicked gleam in his gaze. "Haven't they always been? Hell, they might as well know that Fortune-Rockwell is about to add another partner."

She'd never considered money as being part of the deal. Even though Derek was very well off, he managed not to flaunt his wealth. At least, not here in San Antonio. She'd almost forgotten he wasn't even near normal.

He grabbed her hand and started pulling her toward the closed door.

"Derek…" She laughed, giddy with the touch of him.

Sending her his devilish smirk, he opened the door, bringing her outside, too.

"Looks like everyone's enjoying their lunch hour," he announced jovially.

The crowd shuffled, no doubt embarrassed that their boss was calling them on their nosiness.

But Derek didn't acknowledge the awkwardness. "I thought you'd like to know that she said yes."

Some employees pretended not to know what he was talking about. But Adam, Jonathan, Seth, Ben and Jack all high-fived, causing a relieved chain reaction of applause and felicitations.

· Before anyone could approach them, Christina

gripped Derek's hand and tugged him down the hall toward his office. She wanted to be alone with the man she loved.

Wanted him, period, since there was nothing standing between her and her fiancé now.

Si. Her fiancé.

True love had finally hit her, Christina Mendoza, the unluckiest target of love to ever exist.

They passed Twyla, who was leaning against the wall while excited chatter filled the room. The blonde was sending Christina a jaded look, one that seemed to say, "We both know better, don't we?"

But Christina only held tighter to Derek's hand, feeling the rough skin of his palm brush against hers, creating sparks. Flames.

For a split second, Christina imagined Rebecca Waters's face superimposed over Twyla's. The frowns merged together, morphing into one bad memory.

But, then, unruffled, Christina walked right past, leaving them both behind.

When they arrived at Derek's office, he dismissed Dora, who was eating a sandwich at her desk while surfing the Internet.

"In fact," Derek said to her, "why don't you just take the rest of the day off."

Dora jumped out of her chair. "This job gets better and better!"

Then she took off, and Derek locked the door to

his small lobby, turning around to find his newly minted fiancée leaning against his desk.

Christina.

A fiery flush had stamped her cheeks, bringing a beautiful shine to her eyes and skin.

His wife. His future.

"Should we call Patrick? My parents?" Her smile lit up the room. "Two engagements in the space of days. Mama and Papa are going to hit the roof."

"What about your bet?" he asked, slowly walking away from the door. "Is this going to mess it up?"

"Terribly. I'm toast, Derek. But I'm betting you'll be worth all the heinous work I'll be performing for this lapse into man temptation."

"I'll help you through it."

He was standing in front of her now, coaxing her hair back with his fingers, taking her in as if she'd disappear.

But she wouldn't. This woman would always be around to rescue him from facing more lonely, soulless nights.

"Let's make the phone calls later," he said. "We've got a lot of work to do."

"Work?" She seemed highly disappointed. "You're kidding, right? Because if you're not, I'm really quitting this time."

"A wife can't quit her and her husband's company."

"I'm not your wife yet."

Derek scooped Christina into his arms. "Yes, you

are. The minute you said you loved me, I became your husband."

Molding her body against him, Christina rested her lips against his neck, communicating with a language of kisses. "You move fast, Mr. Rockwell."

"I know a good deal when I see it." He memorized her back with an opened palm, easing over the line of her spine, the curve of her rear end. "They say I'm ruthless when it comes to getting what I want."

"Then show me."

With tender persuasion, he caught her mouth with his, kissing her, slowly exploring her lips, taking his sweet time.

Now, he wasn't afraid to take her inside of him, to let her all the way into a place no one else had ever ventured before. He absorbed the love she was willing to give, allowing it to make him stronger.

Not weaker.

As her kisses burned his skin, searing him with what he once perceived to be wounds, he felt himself healing under her touch, her care.

He lowered her to the carpet, spreading out her hair like an exotic fan, tracing his fingers over her breasts, watching as they peaked, straining against her red shirt.

"I've got that blanket in the closet," he said. "Let me get it."

She pulled him back down to her, and he didn't even mind being restrained.

"I'm comfortable just the way we are," she said.

He had a vision of the red shawl, the way it'd covered her, protected her, bringing out the deeper feelings he'd been repressing.

"I don't want you to be just *comfortable*." He got up, hating to lose the heat between them. But he'd be right back, restoking it. "I want you to know I'm always thinking of you, whether it's a blanket under your back or a far grander gesture. Rose petals over your skin, a trip to a first-class Paris hotel…"

"I just need you," she said. "Not the trimmings."

"Humor me."

Playfully, she stretched out on the floor, Cleopatra-like. "You come right back in record time."

As she sent him a lazy, kiss-warmed smile, Derek's pulse slammed against his skin. He made fast work of fetching the blanket, then made sure he had a condom ready to go.

He spread the heavy, silky material on the floor, then moved over to her, relieving her of her sandals, sliding his fingers over her delicate ankle while urging her body over to him.

"Your office seems like a forbidden place to make love in," she said, voice light, teasing.

"It's been my fortress. And…" He reached over to guide her shirt over her head, leaving her in a lacy white bra. "…you've stormed it."

They slicked off the rest of their clothes until she was in her underwear and he was bare-chested, wearing only his jeans.

Making love in his office would be the statement

of all statements. He was changing the tone of it, announcing to himself that work was nothing compared to this woman.

As Derek lay his body over hers, kissing her once again, business fell by the wayside.

Instead, he lavished fingertip praise on the tops of her breasts, which were mounded by the confines of her bra. With easy strokes, he shaped them, making her shiver, her breath quicken.

Inspired, he dipped his thumb into the cup of her bra, tracing the nipple, round and round, taunting it into arousal.

She reached down between them, caressing him, bringing him to a stiff, aching erection.

Soon, all their clothes littered the floor, and she'd worked the condom over his length, wriggling her hips and lulling him inside, where he slid, drove, pulsated into her.

Together, they danced forward, avoiding the backtracking they'd been doing for most of their lives. They followed their own footsteps this time, not the ones other people had laid out for them.

With rhythmic grace, they explored new ground, forging their own path, seeking mountaintops, peaks, summits.

As Derek got higher and higher with Christina matching every climb in elevation, moaning, gyrating, soaring with him, the pressure built in his body.

It stopped his heart, dizzied his head, stole his oxygen. When his partner climaxed beneath him, crying out her love, helping him reach the top, too, Derek finally burst into pieces, overwhelmed by where they'd gone.

Where they'd go every day for the rest of their lives.

Spent, Derek held Christina to him, their skin slick, melting into each other, fusing two into one.

Then he looked at her, replenishing himself with the woman who'd stolen his energy in the first place. She smiled up at him, a tear of sweat trickling down her face, meandering between her lips like a moist kiss.

He fit his mouth to hers, tasting the salt of it.

Drinking her in.

His wife. His partner.

His elixir.

Epilogue

When Patrick Fortune had received the call from Derek, announcing his engagement to Christina, he'd already been on his way back to Texas from New York, planning to personally congratulate Jack and Gloria on their own upcoming nuptials.

And, now, with the success of The Sequel, Patrick felt doubly blessed.

When he'd learned about the office rumors dogging Christina and Derek, guilt had overshadowed Patrick. But his employees had handled the strife beautifully themselves. Then again, they were both the best, so he wouldn't have expected anything less of them.

However, wanting to make up for his absence,

Patrick had hightailed it to the Mendoza house, which had been host to one big party ever since two out of three daughters had gotten engaged. All week, Patrick had toasted their love, eaten Jose's marvelous food and enjoyed the comfort of family.

But on this weekend, the Mendoza sisters were celebrating Christina's engagement in a different way.

As Patrick's driver dropped him off at the Blinko Gas Station near Stocking Stitch, Maria's knitting store in Red Rock, he caught wind of the festivities: loud laughter, jokes, the lively recorded music of acoustic guitars and the spray of water.

Drawing closer, Patrick adjusted his glasses. Yes, it was true. Just as Gloria had promised, she'd constructed signs that were flapping in the breeze as the Mendozas gathered around a boom box and a cooler of colas and snacks. At the same time, they poked fun at Christina as she washed cars.

Vehicles were lined up on the street, the occupants joining in the fun, calling out to Christina every so often. She'd return the jesting while squirting Jack with water or inviting Sierra to come out and join her.

Labor Of Love! read one sign.

Christina Fought Cupid And Cupid Won! said another.

Another sign, less clever by far, but more meaningful, boasted the words: Car Wash, $10, For Charity. Proceeds Go To The Pediatric Ward Of Red Rock General Hospital.

Patrick wouldn't advertise it, but he'd chip in a few stacks of bills, too. But, just to get into the spirit, he'd allow Christina to work for it.

After all, she *had* lost the bet.

When he walked up, the crowd let out a raucous cheer.

"Sit down and watch the show!" Pregnant, yet still slim, Gloria was happy to squash Christina's shyness with a very public reckoning. Like royalty, she was seated in a lawn chair under an umbrella.

Jack came over to offer his father a cola. Ice chips flaked off the bottle in the spring sun. "Glad you could watch this spectacle, too, Dad."

They made Patrick comfortable in his own chair near Maria and Rosita. While Christina trooped around in her tennis shoes and grubby, wet shorts and shirt, soapy sponge and hose in hand, a dark head popped up from the other side of the car she was washing.

"Is Derek allowed to be helping?" Patrick asked.

Petite Rosita was using a hand-painted fan to cool herself off. "There are so many waiting cars that the Committee for Man Temptation is allowing it."

"Jack, Jose and Sierra are talking about helping, also," Maria said, looking so very pleased about finding two of her daughters their perfect mates. "There is a much bigger turnout than we expected."

Patrick watched as Derek ambled by Christina,

smearing her cheek with bubbles. In retaliation, she sprayed him. When he stopped the attack by enfolding her in a bear hug and kissing her senseless, the observers clapped, urging them on.

"Christina!" yelled Gloria. "I think Sierra took her ring-sitting duties too seriously and ran away with it!"

That got instant attention.

On the sidelines, Sierra was flashing the diamond jewelry at her sister, pretending as if she would take off.

While Derek made to pursue Sierra, Christina held him back, saying how much she trusted her younger sibling. Appeased, Derek resumed work along with his fiancée. But that didn't keep them from casting flirty glances at each other.

Patrick noticed Sierra's own gaze lingering on the ring. A deep loneliness filled her eyes, and it broke his old heart.

"Got any ideas?" Maria asked, noticing his focus.

He turned to her and Rosita, who were on the edges of their seats, anticipating his response.

"Give me some time to think about it," he said, relaxing back into his own. "Just give me some time."

And, with that, his eye turned back to his latest successful merger.

Between his good friends' daughter.

And the son of his heart.

What a team, thought Patrick, only too happy to help out.

Still, he wondered if maybe his best work was yet to come.

* * * * *

Look for the conclusion of
the Mendoza sisters' stories
when the Fortunes of Texas: Reunion *continues*
in April 2005 with
IN A TEXAS MINUTE
by Stella Bagwell.

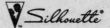

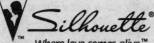

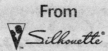

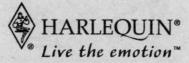